THE TIP-OFF . . .

Slattery,

Stranger just rode in. Spooky tall. Bought himself a Colt double-action .44-40, holster and gunbelt from Tolliver. Wearing a brown hat and brown tweed coat and pants under his slicker. Clean-shaven except for a well-greased longhorn mustache. He says he's on the owl hoot trail, but he asks too damn many questions. Says his name is Long. Smells like a lawman to me.

Thought you ought to know.

Em.

Slattery crumpled the note and flung it into the fire.

Jesus. Simmons had been right. That son of a bitch didn't go down after all, which meant that was Pete the herd pounded into hamburger. And now the bastard was waiting for him in Horsehead. He'd felt it from the first. This son of a bitch was trouble. Big trouble.

* * *

This title includes an exciting excerpt from *Sixkiller* by Giles Tippette. Follow the further adventures of Justa Williams in defending his family from a band of wild cutthroats! Available in May from Jove Books.

TABOR EVANS

LONGARM

AND THE
GUNSLICKS

JOVE BOOKS, NEW YORK

LONGARM AND THE GUNSLICKS

A Jove Book / published by arrangement with
the author

PRINTING HISTORY
Jove edition / April 1992

ISBN: 0-515-10832-4

Jove Books are published by The Berkley Publishing Group,
200 Madison Avenue, New York, New York 10016.
The name "JOVE" and the "J" logo
are trademarks belonging to Jove Publications, Inc.

Chapter 1

Longarm stopped by the clerk's desk. The pink-cheeked youth looked up from his newfangled typewriter machine and grinned. He knew something Longarm didn't.

"Good morning, Mr. Long."

"Billy in?"

"Yep. And he ain't alone."

"That so?"

"He's got a gent in there with him, come all the way from the Washington office."

"In that case, think maybe I'll go on back downstairs for another cup of coffee."

The door to Marshal Billy Vail's office swung open and Vail appeared in the doorway. "It's about time, Longarm. Get in here. We been waitin' for you to show."

Longarm strode past Vail into the marshal's office. Vail closed the door behind him and introduced Longarm to a tall, gangling gent who went by the name of Gus Coleman. He looked about fifty-five or sixty, and his face was the texture and shade of well-worn leather, but his handshake was bony and powerful, and the squint in his eyes said he came from the state of Texas, where the sun glancing off the high plains made it impossible to see any distance without squinting. He was dressed in a dark suit and a white broadcloth shirt with a string tie knotted at his throat. His white Stetson hung on Vail's hat rack in the corner.

"Sit down, Longarm," Vail said. "This here gent's come a long way to meet you."

Gus Coleman chuckled. "All the way from Washington, Mr. Long," he said. "And I was never so happy to put a place behind me. Washington is a damp, dismal swamp of a place and all of it wrapped in red tape."

"That's what I hear," Longarm said, pulling a wooden chair over and setting it down beside Vail's desk. Coleman was using Vail's Moroccan leather arm chair. Longarm offered Coleman a cheroot. The man took it gratefully.

After both men were lit up, Longarm leaned back in his chair. "What have you got for me, gents?"

"A tough one," Vail said.

"There's a man I want you to go after," said Coleman.

"Who're we talking about?"

"A man named Jack Hawkins," said Coleman.

"Never heard of him."

"He won't be going by that name. Not now. He's a renegade peace officer who once served under me when I ran the marshal's office out of Austin."

"When was that?"

"Ten years ago."

2

"And you're still after him?"

"I am," he replied grimly. "A year ago the Washington office got word from an informant that Hawkins had come to roost somewhere in the Montana Territory."

"And now you want me to go after him?"

"It's not that simple, Mr. Long."

"I'm listening."

"In the past year, I've sent two U.S. deputy marshals up there after him—and each one has disappeared without a trace."

"No trace at all?"

"None. That's pretty wild country, still. And what little I've found out points to the fact that Hawkins is a foreman on one of the ranches up there and has gathered around himself a small army of gunslicks. He appears to own the local sheriff and the only town close by."

"That should make him a pretty big target. Easy to spot."

"It also makes him difficult if not impossible to pin down or indict. The Washington office wants him off the books and told me to forget about him. He's an embarrassment to them. They can't keep on sending good men up there and having them disappear."

Vail stirred. "It don't look so good, Longarm. Not to them pencil pushers, anyway."

Longarm took a drag on his cheroot. Hell, it didn't look so good to him, either. This outlaw was beyond the statute of limitations; and the way it looked to Longarm, Coleman's superiors in Washington felt here was no sense in losing any more men over a dead issue. More than likely, they figured Coleman was conducting a personal vendetta.

Which, of course, he was.

"I'm curious," Longarm said to Coleman. "Why do you want this gent so bad?"

Coleman hesitated for only a moment. "Before Hawkins took off, the son of a bitch . . . killed my wife and son."

Longarm glanced quickly over at Vail. Vail's round, pasty face was grim. Longarm looked back at Coleman.

"Would you mind telling me a little more?"

Coleman took a deep breath. "My wife and son entered the Wells Fargo Express office about the same time Hawkins was looting a payroll shipment he was supposed to be guarding. When Hawkins opened up on me, my wife and boy got caught in his line of fire. When I saw them go down, I was in no condition to prevent him from escaping." Coleman paused a moment. "I know now he cut them down deliberately. He knew it would stop me long enough to allow him to get away."

From the lines on Coleman's face Longarm could tell that his recollection of that grim event ten years ago still caused the man considerable pain. Vail cleared his throat.

"Custis, Gus wants you to go in and get that bastard."

"I thought Washington wanted to wash their hands of Hawkins."

"They do."

"I don't want you to go in as a U.S. deputy," Coleman said.

"Let me get this straight," Longarm said. "You want me to leave my badge here?"

4

Coleman nodded. "And if you find Hawkins, I don't see any need for you to bring him back with you."

Longarm looked at Coleman. He didn't want Hawkins brought back dead or alive. He just wanted him dead. Blazing out of the old lawman's eyes was a terrible, implacable hatred—which made it pretty clear why he had journeyed this far to enlist Vail and Longarm in his private vendetta. It didn't matter how Longarm managed it, and there would be no questions asked.

Longarm wanted no part of it.

He shook his head. "Sorry, Mr. Coleman, but I'm no assassin. I'm a lawman."

Coleman sighed deeply, glanced wearily at Vail, then slumped back in his armchair. "I must admit," he said. "I'm not surprised. Billy told me you wouldn't do it."

"Any suggestions, Longarm?" Vail asked.

Longarm thought a moment, then shrugged. "No reason why I couldn't go up there without a badge and poke around awhile. From what you tell me, this bastard is more than likely up to something illegal. Rustling, maybe. Or murder. I could see what develops and bring him back with a fresh charge, one that would stand up in court."

Sudden hope gleamed in Coleman's eyes. "You think you could do that, Mr. Long?"

"Longarm can if anyone can," Vail assured Coleman.

"I'll just need a few more details," Longarm said. "I'd like to see those reports that place him in Montana Territory."

"Of course," said Coleman. "Of course. When could you leave?"

"Depends. Tomorrow, I guess."

"I'd go with you, Mr. Long," Coleman assured him. "But that bastard was always more than a match for me—and I'd only hold you back."

"And he might recognize you."

"Yes, I agree. There's that to consider as well."

"This Hawkins gent, he got any distinguishing characteristics? I know it's been ten years, but it would help if I had some idea of what he looked like."

"I've brought his whole file with me," Coleman replied, pulling a large brown case off Vail's desk, "but back in Texas he was about my height, with thinning, reddish hair. His hair might be gone now, but one thing he'll still have."

"What's that?"

"A long, puckered knife scar running down the inside of his left arm. A bowie knife put it there."

"Can he use the arm all right?"

"Never seemed to give him any trouble that I could see."

Coleman untied and opened the bulky file envelope he had set down beside his chair and handed a photograph to him. The picture was brown at the edges and considerably faded, but it showed a young hard case in a black, flat-brimmed sombrero, looking into the sun, his lean face taut, his eyes squinting. There was no smile on his face.

It didn't look like Jack Hawkins had ever learned to smile.

The day had been cold and wet. And as dusk fell, it threatened to get colder and wetter still. Longarm braced himself against a sudden gust of wet, stinging wind. Astride his mount deep in the Absorokas, he reached a windswept crest and reined in, hunching forward in his saddle while he pulled the collar of his sheepskin jacket closer about his neck.

Before him he saw a trail that ran along the spine of a ridge that led deeper into the high mountain flanks enclosing him. He urged his mount on through the howling wind and followed the trail for almost a mile before it began a long, gradual descent toward the shadows of a distant canyon. Soon the canyon's walls closed in on him. He kept on and came upon a swift, icy mountain stream. He followed it until it vanished into a giant cleft in the rock face to his right.

He kept on, his descent gradual but steady—like the road into hell, he thought—the only sound that of his horse's iron-shod hooves striking the rocky trail. Night fell. The rain lessened, then ceased. A bright silver dollar of a moon sailed into view from behind a fleet of scudding clouds. Glancing about him, Longarm found that the canyon's steep walls had fallen away.

He kept on. The sound of his mount's hooves were muffled now by thick grass. He had outdistanced the wind and left it howling among the towering peaks behind him. Unbuttoning his jacket, he thumbed his hat back off his forehead as he drank in the fresh, pungent aroma of the spring valley opening up before him. His spirits rose.

He left the trail and cut through a moonlit patch of timber, holding to a spiny ridge for a short while before plunging down a few steep draws to a lower valley. Leaning back in his saddle to ease his mount's load, he sniffed like a healthy wild animal at the sharp tangy odor of pine. In less than a day or so, he figured, he would reach the broad valley he had glimpsed from a pass that afternoon. Now, on all sides of him, flowed broad parks and meadowlands washed in pale moonlight.

These lush foothills, he knew, were once the homeland of the Crow and Shoshones. They had lost it all—first to the horse soldiers, then, finally and irrevocably, to the settlers and cattlemen who piled in after the buffalo had been decimated. Longarm thought he could understand how those Indians must have felt—and must still feel.

The clink of shod hooves broke into his thoughts.

He turned his head and saw a dark cloud of horsemen swarming down on him from a stand of timber above him. He pulled his mount around to face them, but decided against reaching for his Colt. There were too many, and, judging from the grim, silent manner of their approach, they had probably already drawn their weapons.

Their leader—a powerful man with a reddish, drooping mustache and coal black eyes—put his horse alongside Longarm's. A slack-jawed rider with a long, narrow snout and yellow teeth kept pace with the him. Both men had unlimbered their sidearms, and their bores stared ominously at Longarm.

"Who the hell are you, mister?" the big man demanded.

"Name's Long. Custis Long. What's yours?"

"Slattery. But I reckon you already know that."

"Hell, I don't know you. Never saw you before in my life."

"That mean you ain't goin' to admit to what you're doing up here in these hills?"

"It's a free country, ain't it?"

"I asked you a question."

Longarm shrugged. "I'm ridin' through."

"That's your story?"

"It happens to be the truth."

By this time the rest of the riders had circled them and were gazing on Longarm with all the tender concern of a sky full of turkey buzzards. Longarm figured there were more than a dozen riders in all.

"No sense in wastin' any time on this one, boss," said his slackjawed companion. "He ain't gonna tell us nothing. None of them others did, either. But that don't matter. He's the hard case them fool stockmen been threatening to bring in."

"I don't know what the hell you men are talking about," Longarm said. "I'm no hired gunslick. I told you, I was just passin' through."

"Maybe you are just passin' through and maybe you ain't," said Slattery. "But I can't take any chances." He glanced at his partner. "Take his hogleg, Pete."

Pete reached over, his saddle leather creaking, and lifted Longarm's Colt from his open holster. Longarm had decided against using his cross-draw rig on this job and had tucked his derringer into the back of his boot. He offered no argument as Pete stuck Longarm's .44 in his own belt. Pete dismounted, unbuckled Longarm's gun belt and used it to bind his hands to the saddlehorn, after which he looped Longarm's reins around his saddlehorn and mounted up again.

"Good-bye, Long," said Slattery, pulling his horse back. "We might be making a mistake. If we are, I'm real sorry."

Slattery turned to Pete. "You know how to handle this?"

9

Pete nodded, and his yellow grin gleamed in the dark night. Then he yanked Longarm's horse after him and spurred through the ring of riders, heading further down the valley, keeping high on the south slope.

Watching them ride off, Slattery felt a little better. The moment he had ridden up to this Custis Long, he had sensed trouble—deep trouble. The poor son of a bitch might be as innocent as he claimed, but that was hard to believe—and besides, there was too much at stake to risk taking any chances now.

Pete and Longarm rode a mile or so before they came within sight of a large trail herd bedded down for the night on the valley floor beneath them. A thousand head at least, Longarm figured. They were from Oregon more than likely, fresh breeding stock hazed over the mountains to swell the local stockmen's herds. The drover's campfires glowed brightly on the valley's sloping flanks on either side of the trail herd. Pete promptly cut down the slope toward the herd and kept abreast of its left flank for a while until he came out ahead of it. Then he cut down onto the valley floor in front of the herd.

Abruptly, the slopes above and behind them came alive with gunfire. Looking back, Longarm saw the night alive with gunflashes as Slattery and his men stormed down upon the herd. As if they were one massive, multihooved beast, the cattle bolted to their feet and charged headlong down the valley—thundering straight for Longarm and Pete.

Longarm's reins were still wrapped about Pete's saddlehorn as Pete kept them directly in the path of the stampeding herd. He glanced back at Longarm, grinning. His intentions were not hard to figure: in a moment he would drop Longarm's reins and let the herd overtake him. Longarm redoubled his efforts to pull himself free and pulled with all his might on his bound wrists. He felt the gunbelt give some, then yanked again. The bones in his wrist cracked—but one hand pulled free. Loosened, the gunbelt whipped off the saddlehorn and vanished into the night. Holding on to the saddlehorn with his left hand, Longarm reached back into his boot for the derringer.

Pete glanced back at Longarm. This time there was a revolver in his hand. Pete fired. Longarm ducked; the round hummed over his head as he swung up his derringer and emptied both barrels at Pete.

Pete vanished from his saddle.

Longarm's horse struck the downed rustler and stumbled, then lurched forward onto its knees. Longarm tumbled over its neck. The night sky whirled about his head. His back struck the turf hard, knocking the wind out of his lungs. He glanced back. The herd was close enough now for him to hear their horns clicking.

Longarm's horse lurched to its feet. He grabbed its trailing reins and vaulted into the saddle, then lashed the horse on ahead of the herd. As soon as he had gained enough speed, he worked his way out of the herd's path, and then he spurred up the valley's flank. Glancing back, he saw—less than twenty yards below him—the gleaming backs of the crazed steers as they plunged on past him.

He drove his mount hard, heading for the timber above him. Once he reached it, he jumped off his mount and pulled it after him into the pines. He kept on up through the trees on foot until he reached a rocky outcropping that gave him an unobstructed view of the valley below. What he saw was the last of the stampeding herd vanishing from sight—and behind it a few bedraggled riders milling fruitlessly: the herd's hapless drovers, more than likely.

Longarm swung back up onto his saddle and rode off the ridge, hoping to find a pass that would take him through this range. He should have felt himself ill-used and to a degree he did. But what he felt more than resentment was a quiet triumph. He was almost certain he had already found Jack Hawkins, the man Gus Coleman had been trying to nail for the past ten years.

He was ten years older and a little heavier in the face, but this was the same squinting, hard-eyed character whose photograph he had seen for the first time in Vail's office.

Only now he called himself Slattery.

Chapter 2

By noon of the next day Longarm was once more passing through a high labyrinth of rock and canyons that twisted and fell off, then angled and tumbled back upon themselves. It was a gray, sunless day, and Longarm was once again riding into a raw wind that smelled of rain. He was following a game trail he had hoped would lead him down from these windswept crags, but as he rode on it almost seemed to him that he would never be released from the cold embrace of these rugged peaks, that he would be doomed to remain forever in the grasp of these towering mountains.

But by midafternoon he could tell he was traveling down a decided incline. Soon he saw thin timber opening up on the slope below the trail, and beyond that, heavier brush and timber. Finally he was free of the cold mountain walls, and through a gap in the rainy mist he glimpsed a dark, wide valley carpeted with the cold green of pines and junipers. He had come at last to that valley he had glimpsed earlier.

The game trail petered out amidst a tumble of foothills, and Longarm kept to the valley floor, where he picked up a muddy, rutted road. Following it, he kept on down the valley, and close on to nightfall, wearing his slicker against the persistent light drizzle, he came in sight of a bleak, nondescript town made up for the most part of unpainted shacks and log cabins, with only a few false-fronted buildings lining its single main street.

He rode into the town and kept on down the main drag until he came to the livery stable. He led his horse into the barn and gave it over to a towheaded kid. He told the kid to grain the animal and rub it down good, reminding him that the horse had taken him a long way through a cold rain. Then he asked if there was a place in the stable where he could stow his saddle and gear. The kid pointed to a door leading to the grain room and said Longarm could stow his gear in there.

"This town have a gunsmith?" Longarm asked.

"Yep," the boy said.

He stepped out through the wide barn door and pointed to a narrow gunsmith shop down the street wedged in between the smithy and the largest building in town, the General Goods and Grain Emporium. Longarm flipped the kid a coin, then stowed his bedroll and gear in the grain room. A moment later, head down, he was slogging through the rain on his way to the gunsmith's shop. Inside it, he selected a .44-40 double-action Colt. He hefted it to get some idea of its balance, then loaded it and asked the gunsmith if he could take it out back to test it.

14

The gunsmith had no objection, and Longarm returned a few moments later, satisfied. The gun pulled slightly to the left, but he was able to compensate for that easy enough, and he liked the weapon's heft. He purchased a new gunbelt and holster to go with it and a box of shells. He strapped on the gun, and, without haggling, paid the gunsmith.

"What town is this, mister?" he asked.

"Horsehead," the man replied, ringing up the sale.

This was it then, the town Longarm had been searching for. He was wearily gratified to have found it in the midst of all this weather. He left the shop and walked back through the thin, chill rain until he reached what appeared to be the town's largest saloon, The Horsehead.

Shouldering through the saloon's batwings, he found the place long, narrow, and not too well lighted. The sawdust on the floor hadn't been lightened in a day or so, at least. He ordered a beer and took it over to a table in the corner. A game of poker was in progress, and two very serious drinkers were nursing their shot glasses at two other tables. That was about all the business in the place. Idly sipping his beer, Longarm nudged his hat back off his forehead and tipped his chair back against the wall. It felt good to have something solid under his rump for a change.

A woman came from the back and walked up to the bar. She was in her late thirties. Her lips and cheeks were rouged, but it didn't do much to tighten the fleshy contours of her face or soften her mouth's cold line. She had combed out her rust-colored hair so it rested on her shoulders and her long, bottle-green dress accentuated her full bust and narrow waist. The most attractive thing about her was her eyes. They were slanted slightly and were a soft emerald green.

When she spotted him sitting alone, she asked the barkeep something and approached his table.

"Stranger in town?" she asked.

"Yep," Longarm replied.

"Do you like to drink alone?"

"I hate it, but like I just said, I'm a stranger in town."

She laughed softly. "May I join you?"

"I'd be delighted."

She sat across from him, motioned to the barkeep for a drink, and turned to face Longarm. "My name is Emerald Riley. I own this place."

"Name's Long. Custis Long. Pleased to meet you, Emerald." He looked around the saloon. "How's business?"

"It's a lot better on weekends."

The barkeep brought Longarm another beer—on the house—and Emerald a shot glass of whiskey. Longarm reached gratefully for the beer and took a gulp, wiping the suds off his chin with the back of his hand.

"Where you from, Custis?"

"Do I have to tell you?"

She smiled, but there was no humor behind it. "Course not—just curious, that's all."

Longarm shrugged. "Two weeks ago I was in New Mexico. I found it a much warmer place than this high country. You might say I'm up here to cool off."

She smiled, seemingly relieved. "Some men do find this a good place to cool off," she admitted.

"Only right now I'm pretty flat. Any chance of work around here?"

16

"What kind of work?"

"This is cattle country. I've hazed a few cows in my day."

"You don't look like a cowpoke to me."

"I didn't say I was. A man'll never get rich punching another man's beef. But when it's raining, there's no sense in standing in it with your hat off if you don't have to."

"That's true." She regarded him closely for a moment. "You might try the Lazy C," she said. "Their foreman is always looking for men like you—men who can handle themselves in tight places."

"Is that the kind of man I am."

She smiled and sipped her whiskey. "It's just a feeling I have."

"What's this foreman's name?"

"Slattery. Buck Slattery. Just tell him I sent you."

"I appreciate that, Emerald."

"Just one thing, Custis . . ." She leaned closer, her emerald eyes gleaming.

"What's that?"

"A little word of warning."

"About what?"

"If you're a lawman, you'd be smart to leave this saloon and ride out of here. It ain't healthy for lawmen in this country."

"Now what makes you think I'm a lawman?"

She looked at him coolly, then shrugged. "You don't have the appearance of a man on the run. It's a look I usually recognize. The truth of it is you look like a man too strong to break and too brave to run."

"Much obliged for the compliment. But you might say my looks is what's caused most of my trouble."

He grinned. "People tend to trust me too much."

"All right. I warned you. Now it's up to you."

"Thanks for the warning." He finished his beer and looked around, then back at her. "Say, this town got a hotel?"

"It did have—before it burned down."

"I need a place where I can I bunk for the night."

"Try the restaurant across the street. The owner might let you share her apartment on the second floor. Perhaps even her bed. Her name's Irene."

Longarm raised his eyebrows, obviously interested.

"From what I hear," Emerald went on, "one wink at Irene and you hit the jackpot."

Longarm stood up. "Well then. Guess I'll mosey over there and check out my wink."

He left the saloon. The rain had begun to let up some. The town had no street lamps, so the only light came from the saloon's windows and those of the restaurant on the other side of the street. He slogged through the mud and stepped into the restaurant. It was empty. The smell of mashed potatoes and gravy filled the place. He chose a table near the window, ordered from the hefty blonde he assumed was Irene a steak and mashed potatoes and a side order of green peas, and told Irene to keep the coffee coming. He ate heartily, then beckoned to the waitress. She had been most generous with her portions. The steak was at least two inches thick, and her coffee had been powerful enough to give him a new lease on life. During his solitary meal she had watched over him eagerly and now hurried to his table.

"You want some dessert, mister?"

18

"What've you got?"

"Apple pie."

"Maybe another time. Are you Irene?"

She frowned warily. "Yes."

"Irene, I got a problem."

From the look on her face, he could tell she thought he was going to stiff her for the meal. He smiled quickly to reassure her.

"I just rode in and I need a place to bunk for the night. Emerald said you might have a room upstairs where I could stay."

"Oh," Irene said. "A room. Sure. But it'll cost you."

"How much."

"Counting the meal, five dollars."

"Pretty steep, isn't it?"

"Sleep outside in the rain, then."

"I guess I got no choice."

"That'll be five dollars, in advance."

He paid her and stood up.

"Lead the way."

He followed her through the kitchen, past the Chinese cook, and outside where they mounted a flight of wooden steps. She had an apartment on the second floor which consisted of two rooms. One was furnished as a sitting room and contained a wood stove and a sofa. The other was her bedroom. On its door was a bolt that could be worked only from the sitting room side.

"You may have the bedroom," Irene told him. "I'll sleep in here on the sofa."

"I don't like to be locked in," Longarm said, indicating the bolt.

She shrugged, as if to say that was how it had to be—or no room for the night.

19

All at once, it seemed, he was too exhausted to argue with anyone about anything and he discovered that he had absolutely no desire to wink at her. The big meal had done him in and he was more than ready for sleep. He moved into her bedroom and sat down on the edge of the bed.

She followed him in. "What's your name?"

"Long. Custis Long."

"I'd be gratified if you would plant your boots over there in the corner, Mr. Long. You've left a track of mud clear through my sitting room."

"Sorry about that," he said, tugging off his boots and lugging them over to the corner.

"Well, then," she said. "Good night, Mr. Long."

She turned and left the room, closing the door firmly behind her. He waited for her to shoot the bolt, but all he heard was her footsteps on the outside steps as she went back down to the restaurant. He walked over to the window and was just in time to see the towheaded kid from the livery stable heading out of town, his sheepskin coat and a battered straw sombrero his only protection from the rain. Longarm's gut told him where the towhead was going. Emerald was sending the kid out to the Lazy C to warn Slattery of the stranger who just rode into town.

Longarm went back to his bed and dragged the mattress onto the floor, then kicked it over so it rested against the wall with the bed's brass frame between him and the door. Using both pillows to simulate his sleeping form, he covered them with the bedspread, then lay down on the mattress, his new Colt in hand. The last thing he removed before he fell asleep was his hat.

• • •

Longarm was awake instantly, reaching for his .44.
It was Irene. She had cautiously pushed open his
door and entered the room. She was outlined clearly
in the light from the lamp in her sitting room. Slowly, stealthily, she approached his bed and reached
out to the dummy he had placed on the bed spring.

From below the bed he asked softly, "What are
you doing in here, Irene?"

She uttered a startled cry and jumped back. He
stood up, his .44 still in his hand, its new metal
gleaming in the dim light.

"I came in to warn you," she said, her voice
hushed.

"About what?"

"I been hearing talk. The kid from the stables has
gone after Slattery. He's the Lazy C ramrod. And
the sheriff's heard about you. He wants to know
who you are and what you're doing in this town."

"How come this town gets so uneasy when a new
man rides in?"

"You don't understand."

"What don't I understand?"

"This place ain't like other towns. Men who drift
in here are usually runnin' from the law. Lawmen
who ride in looking for outlaws, they never ride out.
They just disappear."

"That a fact?"

"Yes. It surely is."

"Well now, that suits me just fine."

"You mean you're—"

"I didn't say that," Longarm told her. "So don't
you go jumpin' to any conclusions."

"All right, then. I won't."

21

She looked him up and down, then smiled, almost shyly.

"Why the smile?"

"You look so silly standing in your long johns with that big gun in your hand."

"And you, on the contrary, look very nice in that silk nightgown with all that pink lace and ruffles."

"I don't look too fat?"

"I think you're a lot of woman, that's what I think."

He reached out and pulled her close and knew instantly what he had already suspected: she was wearing nothing under the gown. With a sigh, she leaned against him, resting her head on his chest. She had shampooed and combed out her long golden hair before coming in here to warn him. He had guessed from the start that her warning was simply a pretext for joining him in bed, but he didn't mind; he was pleased, in fact. She was a warm, pleasant woman and the last thing he wanted was for her to know how obvious her stratagem had been.

She lifted her face to glance up at him. Her eyes had gone darker, her pale complexion was flushed. In the dim light that filtered in from her sitting room he saw tiny beads of perspiration on her upper lip.

"You sure I have time for this?" he asked softly. "After what you just told me about the sheriff."

"Don't worry about him. Not now. He won't wake up from his drunken sleep until noon," she said, "and the Lazy C is half a day's ride from here."

"Good," he said. "We have plenty of time."

He kissed her full on the lips. They were moist and pliant, opening eagerly to his probing tongue. It was a long kiss, turning them both molten. She pulled

22

away at last and, reaching back, flung her nightgown over her head. He peeled out of his long johns
almost as fast and pulled her down onto the mattress beside him. Before embracing her again, he
took the time to gaze upon her shimmering naked-
ness. Her breasts were more than ample, her curves
generously rounded, her belly swelling opulently,
her hips arching—and in the dark hollow of her
crotch, her golden pubic hair gleamed like spun gold.

She laughed softly. "Do you like what you see?"

"Indeed I do, ma'am."

"My, aren't we formal."

She opened her arms to him. He bore her down
under him. She spread her legs eagerly and he slipped
into her effortlessly, the moist warmth of her closing
about his erection like hot silk. His big calloused hands
reached under her buttocks and thrust her up at him
as he plunged in still deeper. She gasped and flung
her arms about his neck, nearly choking him. He
bore down heavily, impaling her on his rigid lance;
and with a delighted gasp, she began to rock, her
inner muscles squeezing him, milking him, her head
tossing from side to side, until at last, with a keening
cry that seemed to come from deep in her throat, she
cried out—and he felt her shuddering orgasm as she
came again and again.

Longarm remained inside her, her warm juices
flowing around his erection.

"Oh!" Irene cried. "You're still inside me!"

"Hang on," he said. "I ain't finished yet."

"You're so *big*."

"Yes, ain't I."

He pulled her over gently but firmly until she was
astride him. She was panting eagerly by this time,

her hair cascading like a golden curtain down over her face.

She leaned back and sank still further about his shaft. Reaching up, he stroked her breasts, slowly and gently, circling her nipples with his thumbs, around and around, as she leaned back still further and closed her eyes, moaning softly. Then he slipped his hands caressingly down to hips and thighs. She began to rock back and forth as if she were in the midst of a dream. He looked up through her hair at her parted lips. She licked them drowsily, her breath catching in her throat.

Faster and faster now, she began to rock. She was panting like a she-cougar as her hips began to thrust with maddening insistence back and forth. Longarm reached up and grabbed her hip-bones to keep himself deep. She rode him faster and still faster, all caution thrown to the winds, her breath coming in rapid, panting bursts.

Unable to hold himself back any longer, he swiftly built to his own climax, the urgency of it like a scream in his gut. He hung on to her, his chest heaving, slamming her back and forth with both hands, thrusting her down upon him until at last he arched his back and came in a tremendous rush, carrying her up with him, then down over the precipice.

Laughing, they collapsed in each other's arms, spent, covered with perspiration. Longarm brushed back Irene's damp golden locks and kissed her full on the lips, aware of the musky, nighttime smell of her. The kiss over, she sighed, pushed herself upright and, with a soft "good night," vanished from the room, pulling the door shut behind her. Again, he did not hear her bolt the door.

He reached out for his .44, and with his right hand closed about its butt he dropped back into a deep, contented sleep.

Chapter 3

Slattery heard Sim's cry, looked up from the branding iron, and saw Will Hammer riding toward them. The ground was still wet from a pounding rain, so horse and rider materialized soundlessly out of the damp night. Em must've sent the kid. Dammit. She must have had to tell the kid how to reach this small, hidden valley. Shit. In that case, maybe she had told him too much.

Slattery handed his running iron to Hunnicut and walked out of the ring of fire, missing its warmth at once. The towhead pulled his horse to a halt, swung down, took off his torn, straw sombrero, and brushed a lock of hair off his forehead. Will was about fourteen years old, a gawky, skinny kid who looked to be starving on the pitiful rations the owner of the livery stable allowed him.

"Howdy, Mr. Slattery," he said, glancing nervously at the branding fires winking in the night. He was trying not to notice, Slattery saw, but his kid's curiosity got the better of him.

"Em send you?"

"Yes, sir. She gave me a note for you."

"Let's have it."

The kid dug into his jacket's side pocket and handed Slattery a folded piece of paper.

"Em told you how to get here, did she?"

"Yes, sir, Mr. Slattery."

"Easy to find, was it?"

"No, sir. I got lost twice. But when I topped that ridge up there and looked down and saw them . . . campfires . . . I knew for sure I'd found you."

The kid shivered in the damp night air and pulled the ragged collar of his sheepskin coat closer about his neck.

"Might as well come on over to the fire, get the chill off," Slattery told him, resigned now to the fact that this kid not yet dry behind the ears was going to know all about his operation and there was not going to be a thing he could do about it.

He reached the fire, told the kid to go find some coffee, then leaned close to the flames and read Em's note.

Slattery,

Stranger just rode in. Spooky tall. Bought himself a Colt double-action .44-40, holster and gunbelt from Tolliver. Wearing a brown hat and brown tweed coat and pants under his slicker. Clean-shaven except for a well-greased longhorn mustache. He says he's on the owl hoot trail, but he asks too damn many questions. Says his name is Long. Smells like a lawman to me.

Thought you ought to know.
Em.

Slattery crumpled the note and flung it into the fire.

Jesus. Simmons had been right. That son of a bitch didn't go down after all, which meant that was Pete the herd pounded into hamburger. And now the bastard was waiting for him in Horsehead. He'd felt it from the first. This big son of a bitch was trouble. Big trouble.

"Hey, Sim!" Slattery cried. "Get over here!"

Simmons released the steer he was working on, jumped up, and hurried over. Slattery could smell the stench of singed flesh that still clung to him.

"Yeah, boss?"

"You said you saw Pete go down. Tell me what you saw."

"Well," Sim said, shifting his feet uneasily, "maybe you were right, boss. Maybe I was only seein' things."

"Pete hasn't shown up, has he? We been here two hours now and there's no sign of him. So dammit, what did you see?"

"It was pretty dark so I couldn't see all that good, boss. Pete and the big guy was ridin' hard in front of the herd. I waited for Pete to drop the reins and cut away. Instead I saw a flash of gunpowder and the next thing I knew Pete went over. The stranger went down, too—and then I couldn't see no more. You saw how fast that herd was moving—and them drovers were all over us by that time. Like wet hornets."

"You say they both went down?"

"That's the way it looked to me."

29

No doubt about it. Pete was as dead as last night's poker game. It was just like the stupid son of a bitch. He never had no sense. Always had to use his gun. Not content to let the herd take care of Long, he must've tried to ventilate him first, lost his balance and went over. That stranger must've landed like a cat and somehow ridden out of the herd's path.

"Luke ain't goin' to like this one bit," Slattery said, glancing over at the most distant branding fire.

"Hell," said Simmons, "him and his brother never got on worth a shit, boss."

"Don't matter. They're kin. Go get him, Sim."

"What'll I tell him?"

"Nothing. I'll handle this. And hurry it up. I want to finish this bunch before Billingsly shows up."

As Simmons hurried off, the kid approached Slattery. He was leading his horse.

"Where you goin', kid?"

"Guess I'll be headin' back to town, Mr. Slattery."

"Hell, no," Slattery told him. "You don't have to do that. You ain't gonna ride all the way back there this late. We need you here."

Will looked around him nervously. He knew goddamn well what was going on and wanted to clear out, keep his nose clean.

"Here?"

"Sure, Will. You're working for the Lazy C now."

"Gee, I don't know, Mr. Slattery . . ."

"Hey, think a minute. Ain't that what you want? You rather spend the rest of your life forking horse manure? I'm offerin' full wages. Thirty dollars and found."

The boy considered this sudden, unexpected offer.

"Thirty and found, Mr. Slattery. Full wages?"

"You ain't hard of hearin', are you?"

"No, sir."

"Well?"

"Why, sure, Mr. Slattery. I guess that would be fine with me."

"Good. Grab a running iron and get to work. We got some fancy hides to etch on and not much time to do it. One more thing. You remember a stranger ridin' into Horsehead earlier today."

"I remember."

"Big fellow, was he?"

"He sure was."

"Had a longhorn mustache and cold blue eyes?"

"Yessir, that's the one."

Slattery turned to one of the branding fires. "Hunnicut!" he called. "Take Will in tow here. We got ourselves a new hand!"

As the kid started toward Hunnicut's fire, Slattery took the reins to the kid's mount and led it over to the rope corral. It was there Luke Carson caught up to him.

"Sim says you want to see me, boss."

"Yeah, I do."

"It's about Pete, ain't it."

Slattery hesitated.

"You can tell me," Luke went on. "I know something's wrong. I been watching for him. He should've been here by now. What happened?"

"Looks like he got trampled, Luke. Him instead of that stranger. Simmons saw it. I didn't want to believe it, so I waited. But there's no doubt now— and the man who did it is in Horsehead right now."

"That stranger," Luke said, his face drawn. "He's in Horsehead?"

"He must have managed to ride out of the herd's path."

Luke moistened his lips. "Boss, I want to go after him. Now."

"I guess if I were you I'd feel the same way."

"Where is the son of a bitch stayin'?"

"I don't know. Go see Em when you get in. She might know."

As Luke started for the rope corral to get his horse, Slattery said, "Don't try anything fancy, Luke. Just shoot the son of bitch and be done with it."

"I know what to do, boss."

Luke bulled his way into the rope corral to cut out his mount.

A few moments later, after he watched Luke ride out, Slattery headed back to his fire. He had almost reached it when he caught sight of five riders moving down the slope on the other side of the ravine, scattering freshly branded cattle as they came on. The moon was behind low-hanging clouds, but Slattery had no difficulty picking out the black felt derby hat worn by H. C. Billingsly.

The stock dealer was in the lead; his four drovers keeping their distance behind him. Slattery swore under his breath and walked toward the riders until they were close enough for him to greet. Billingsly dismounted and strode toward him, a broad smile on his beefy face. A powerful man, he was wearing a gray slicker over his dark suit. His thrusting jaw was clean-shaven, his black eyebrows beetling, the eyes under them shifty.

"We been cutting through this herd all the way down the valley," he said approvingly. "This one beats all to hell that last one you brought in."

32

"It's a big one, all right. Ain't that what I told you?"

Billingsly glanced around to take in the size of the gather. Pleased, he looked back at Slattery. "If you ain't too greedy, Slattery, you can leave me enough for an additional agency contract."

Slattery considered a moment. "We still talkin' the same price per head."

"Don't see why not."

"You sure you can swing that? You said it yourself, this is one big herd. There's at least two hundred head more than you bargained for."

"I will give you my IOU for what I owe, and I'll deliver on it in Horsehead in two weeks."

"Done," said Slattery, and the two shook hands.

Billingsly left him then to direct his drovers to help brand the beef Slattery was cutting out for the Lazy C. As Slattery knew, Billingsly had a full crew waiting on the other side of the mountains. They would alter the brands on the culls he was getting from Slattery, which he would then sell to the BIA.

It was a good deal all around.

Slattery moved back to one of the fires to help out in the branding. This trail herd had been his best haul so far. Come fall, the Lazy C range would be solid with tallowed beef, putting him in a position to request a full partnership in the Lazy C—as Rosita Calaveras's husband, something Em was willing to accept.

Rosita's father had been dead for three years now, and it was high time she took herself a husband. That such a woman had not already done so was criminal. Just thinking of those magnificent thighs and breasts sleeping alone kept Slattery awake at night.

He could not see her refusing his offer. They got along well enough, and Slattery had been careful never to push his attention on her. And there was no doubt she admired the way his management of the spread had raised the quality of Lazy C beef. Right now the Lazy C was the most prosperous spread in the valley, and Rosita knew it. She might not like the cowhands he had imported, but she couldn't find fault with much else. As he often told her, it was results that counted.

And with Luke taking out this stranger, it might all come to pass.

Longarm lifted his head and closed his hand tightly about the grip of his .44. He could tell from the stealthy way the door swung open that this wasn't Irene making another visit.

A small wiry figure entered the room. In the darkness, Longarm could not make out his features, but something about the way he moved seemed vaguely familiar. Crouching, the man moved closer to Longarm's bed. The coverlet still covered the pillows he had bunched up and it was at this that the intruder was directing his attention.

His right fist was big with a revolver. Watching from the floor behind the bed, Longarm waited for a clear shot. Besides, he needed to know if this man was alone. Irene had mentioned the sheriff. Apparently, however, this man was in here on his own. With no hesitation, he thrust out his weapon and fired three quick rounds into the pillows Longarm had bunched up. Then he moved still closer, flung aside the coverlet, and fired once more into what he thought was Longarm's head.

In the small room, the four reports boomed like cannon fire. The walls reverberated, and the floor seemed to heave under Longarm. The air was heavy with the acrid stench of gunsmoke. Deliberately, without any wasted motion, Longarm grasped the bed frame and levered his body into position. Catching the motion, the startled gunslick turned to face Longarm. He swung up his revolver. Like a rattler striking from a crevice, Longarm fired point-blank into the intruder's chest. He heard the thunk of lead striking flesh as the little man staggered back and struck the wall.

Dropping his gun, he cried, "Don't kill me! I'm unarmed!"

Longarm lowered his gun and stood up. His would-be assassin slipped crookedly down the wall to the floor. When he hit, his head lolled loosely forward. He looked about as dead as a man can get. Longarm heard the pound of footsteps on the outside steps. A moment later a beefy, round-bellied brute of a man charged through Irene's sitting room and into the bedroom. He was holding his sidearm in his right hand. Longarm had him covered as he entered, and when he saw this, the big man hastily lowered his gun. A tin star was pinned to his greasy vest.

"Guess you'd be the sheriff," Longarm drawled.

"Sheriff Jim Belcher. Now who in hell are you?"

"I'm the man this cockroach came up here to kill."

"I want your name, dammit!" Belcher blustered.

"Custis Long."

The sheriff leaned over to inspect the wounded man. Grabbing a fistful of his hair, he yanked the

35

face up so he could see it, then turned angrily to face Longarm. "Hell! You done killed Luke Carson!"

"That his name, is it?"

Longarm leaned close and studied the man's narrow face. His bullet had plowed into the center of Luke Carson's chest. Frowning, Longarm found himself studying the dead man's long snout, his close-set, liquid eyes. Then he straightened up.

"He looks familiar to me, Sheriff—like someone I met not too long ago. He got any kin in these parts?"

"His brother, Pete."

"And I'll bet they both work for the Lazy C."

Before the sheriff could reply, a loud groan came from the sitting room. Longarm pushed past the sheriff and saw Irene sitting up on her sofa, rubbing her head gingerly. He could tell from the look on her face that she was in considerable pain.

She blinked up at him, squinting. "My head. It hurts."

He leaned close and felt her head gently, coming upon a large and growing lump on the side of her head where Luke Carson had clubbed her while she slept.

"You got a mean crack there, Irene. Luke Carson did it. You better keep still for a while. You might have a concussion."

"A concussion? What's that?"

He laughed. "A bump on the head."

"Oh."

Abruptly, Longarm felt the sheriff's gun barrel pressing into the small of his back. It was not a gentle poke.

"You're under arrest, mister," the sheriff said. "Hand me your gun, grips first."

Longarm straightened cautiously, turned and did as he was told.

"What's the charge?"

"Murder. The murder of Luke Carson."

"Hell, Sheriff! You chewin' on loco weed? Carson came up here to kill me. He knocked out Irene, then crept into my room and started shooting at me. Irene here will testify to that. It was self-defense."

The sheriff smiled coldly. "All right, then. I'm locking you up for discharging a firearm within the town limits . . . and disturbing the peace."

"What about hunting without a license, you stupid son of a bitch?"

"Turn around and march."

"Where to?"

"We got a lockup down the street. Head for it."

Longarm glanced over at Irene. "You going to be all right?"

Still rubbing the side of her head, she nodded, her eyes filled with concern for him.

Longarm marched through the door and out onto the landing, then pulled up. The sheriff bumped into him, his six-gun ramming Longarm painfully.

"Damn it, Sheriff," Longarm snarled, turning as he spoke. "You don't have to stick that gun barrel clean through to the other side, do you?"

Startled, the sheriff took half a step back.

"Never mind that, mister," he blustered. "Just keep on going down them steps."

Instead, Longarm kept turning and slammed his left elbow against the sheriff's gun hand, knocking it aside. Stepping in close then, he rammed his fist deep into the sheriff's soft gut. The man gasped and sagged forward, his eyes bulging out of his head.

For a moment Longarm thought he was going to cry. He dropped his weapon, and Longarm heard it clatter down the wooden steps behind him. Stepping to one side, Longarm grabbed Belcher by the nape of his neck and hurled him down the steps after his revolver.

The sheriff tumbled clumsily, ass over teakettle, and came to rest sprawled face up in a muddy puddle. He had been conscious when he began his descent, but he was out cold when he came to rest. Longarm followed him down the steps, retrieved his .44, and flung the sheriff's own revolver into the darkness. A quick inspection of the unconscious lawman showed him to be breathing in sharp, spasmodic gasps. He had probably suffered nothing more serious than a few cracked ribs.

Longarm headed for the livery, intent on retrieving his gear and saddling up his mount. He had the distinct impression that he had worn out his welcome in Horsehead.

Chapter 4

Rosita Calaveras was seething at the scene below her, but she kept herself under control, bitterly aware that it was her own fault for having given Slattery such a free rein these past two years.

She was tall, almost five-foot-ten, but slim enough to allow a grown man's hands to span her tiny waist. No man had yet tried this, however; she had not seen one she would allow close enough to attempt such an impertinence. Her hair was as black as a raven's wing, her cheekbones sharp, her neck long and graceful. But it was the shimmering gleam of her large, dark, almond-shaped eyes that caused her ranch hands to halt in their work whenever she walked past them.

At the moment she was high on a ridge astride her favorite black. She was dressed in her usual riding habit: a black, flat-brimmed, low-crowned sombrero, a man's black, tight-fitting trousers, exquisitely hand-tooled riding boots, a black vest trimmed in gold thread and beneath it the flash of a white silk shirt. At her throat was a black silk bandanna.

She had been almost twenty when her father died, leaving her in the care of her father's faithful Mexican retainer, Eduardo De Santos, and Blossom, the Shoshone housekeeper and cook her father had slept with at the last. In the years since his death, she had let Buck Slattery and Eduardo run the ranch, content to concentrate almost exclusively on the saddle horses she bred in preference to the smaller mustangs and Indian ponies that abounded in the region.

But it was a long time since her father's death, and she had come to the conclusion that she was old enough to take a more active part in managing the Lazy C. For this reason she had decided earlier to accompany Slattery when he took the Lazy C hands into the foothills to help in the spring roundup. She was anxious to see how her stock had wintered. Eduardo had promised to tell Slattery of her intention to accompany them, but before he could do so, her foreman had pulled out without her.

Annoyed, and still determined to take part in the spring roundup, she had asked Eduardo which range Slattery had selected to begin the roundup. At first Eduardo said he was not sure. But Rosita had persisted and Eduardo had reluctantly directed her into the canyons and high pastures to the north of the ranch. But though she searched diligently, she found no trace of Slattery or any of the Lazy C hands. Curious and not a little puzzled, she had drifted south, staying above the timberline to give herself an extended view of her range. She found Lazy C cattle everywhere, and was pleased to see that most of them had lasted through the winter in good shape. But there was no sign at all of Slattery and the Lazy C hands. She spent the nights camping out under the stars and the days rounding up small gathers, which she hazed down to the lusher, spring-fed pastures further below.

Returning finally to the ranch, she pressed Eduardo for information about her foreman's whereabouts. This time she could not help but notice how nervous he became at her insistent questioning. So she pulled back and bided her time. She did not have long to wait. The day following her return, Eduardo rode out just before dawn without telling her where he was going.

Saddling her black, Rosita followed him.

It was full daylight now as she looked down upon her Lazy C riders and watched them haze long files of cattle ahead of them into the draws and arroyos above the valley floor. It was obvious that this was where Slattery intended them to remain until it was safe to drive them down into the valley, where they could be mixed in with Lazy C's wintered stock. Earlier, in a draw about a mile back, she had come upon a small gather of the rustled steers. She had dismounted and inspected in astonishment their raw, freshly-singed brands.

Now she watched as Eduardo and Slattery, astride their mounts, conversed close by a canyon wall. She was sure they were discussing her, or more precisely, the fact that she had ridden off to find Slattery and, unable to find him, obviously suspected something. But Rosita no longer suspected. She knew. Her foreman Buck Slattery was a cattle rustler—and Eduardo, a man she had looked upon almost as a father, was in league with him!

A few minutes earlier, Rosita had watched five riders drive off a fairly large herd, heading southwest. Slattery had shaken the hand of one of them, a man wearing a slicker and a derby hat, obviously closing a deal. She knew what this meant. Slattery had just sold a portion of the rustled cattle to the man in the derby hat. After all, why should he be above lining his own pockets?

It was now painfully clear to her what had been going on since Slattery took over as foreman, why the Lazy C's burgeoning prosperity was arousing such enmity from the other ranchers in the area— and why the men Slattery had hired to ride for the Lazy C brand were so hated and feared. What she had long refused to allow herself to believe, she could no longer deny.

The Lazy C was being run by an outlaw, and her riders were outlaws as well—gunslicks imported by her foreman.

A fly lit on her black's ear. The high-strung animal snorted angrily and gave his powerful head an impatient shake. The sudden movement appeared to catch the attention of a Lazy C rider below her. Rosita swiftly drew the black off the ridge, swung it about, and headed at a fast gallop back to the Lazy C, her thoughts racing. She needed time to swallow her fury and gain some measure of control over her ranch. But she had no idea how she could accomplish this.

And what hurt the most was the knowledge that Eduardo was a part of it.

• • •

Slattery reached over to pat the neck of his restless mount. "You worry too much, Eduardo," he told the old man.

"But I tell you, Señor Slattery, Rosita suspects something."

"Of course she does. It's about time she began asking questions. Go on back to the ranch. Say nothing to her. Let me tell her. Hell, she'll see things our way. We've given her a cattle kingdom second to none in these parts, the equal of the one them Texans took away from her father."

The suns of sixty years had tanned Eduardo's lined face to the consistency of old leather. "Yes, it is true," he said. "Our ranges, they are fat with sleek beef. But all this we have done with rustled cattle. I do not think Rosita will allow such a thing."

"Hey, Eduardo. You worry too much. Name a rancher who hasn't helped himself to a few mavericks now and then."

"A few, yes, but Señor Slattery, you have turned entire herds into mavericks."

"That I have, Eduardo. You put it very well."

The old man shrugged unhappily. "And I do not think Rosita will like me for what I have let you do."

"Don't worry. I'll make it clear you had no choice. Relax, Eduardo. I've watched Rosita on them horses she breeds. Hell, all we've done is give her the chance to spend more money on her fancy horseflesh. She ain't going to mind that one bit."

Hunnicut rode over to them and waited for a chance to speak.

"What is it, Hunnicut?" Slattery said, turning to face him.

Hunnicut nudged his mount closer. "I saw a rider up there on the ridge just now."

Slattery glanced up at it, then back at Hunnicut. "You sure of this?"

Hunnicut nodded.

"Did you get a good look?"

"Yes, I did, boss. It was a woman forking a black."

Eduardo swore softly.

Slattery said, "You think you might know who it was?"

Hunnicut nodded unhappily. "It was Miss Rosita, boss."

"All right, Hunnicut. Thanks."

Slattery watched Hunnicut ride back to the other riders still hazing the cattle, then patted his horse's neck thoughtfully. "Shit, Eduardo. You led Rosita right to us."

"You see? I told you she was suspicious."

"If you knew that, you should have been more careful riding out here. This sure as hell complicates matters. I wanted to break the news to her in my own time—in my own way. Now the fat's in the fire."

"I am sorry, Señor Slattery. I did not think she would follow me."

"Stay here with the men. Keep them busy. I think I'm going to have to go after Rosita and explain things right now."

Eduardo seemed ready to refuse—as if he preferred to be the one who went after Rosita instead of Slattery. But he said nothing, pulled his horse around and followed after Hunnicut. The white-haired old

44

man rode ramrod straight in his saddle, his right arm hanging down past his thigh—a tiresome, meddling retainer Slattery knew now he should have taken care of long before this.

He clapped spurs to his mount and lifted his horse to a quick run on a course that would take him out through the draw and up onto that ridge. He was hoping he could overtake Rosita before she arrived back at the ranch.

Rosita was within sight of the Lazy C when Slattery's shout alerted her. She glanced over her shoulder and saw him topping a rise. Frowning in annoyance, she slowed the black, then turned it to face him as he galloped down the long swale.

When he yanked his mount to a halt beside her, he said, "You were back there in the hills. I reckon you saw the cattle."

"You mean the cattle you rustled."

Slattery shrugged. "Have it your way. But them cows is wearing our brand now. What's done is done."

"Maybe so, Mr. Slattery, but I still have a recourse."

"What's that, Miss Rosita."

"You're fired, Slattery. Go on to the ranch for your gear, then keep on going."

Slattery swallowed, somewhat off balance. This conversation wasn't going at all the way he had figured it would. At that moment he was depressingly aware of how much he had misjudged Rosita.

"What about my men?"

"I want them gone, too. They're gunslicks you imported."

"They're loyal Lazy C hands."

"No, they're loyal to you. Not to the Lazy C. Don't bother to deny it."

Slattery shrugged unhappily. "They're tough men, Miss Rosita. You need them in this valley—and you need me, too."

"I need you and your men like I need the cholera," she snapped.

"Well now, let's not go so fast," Slattery replied, hearing his voice become heavy and threatening, despite his effort to keep himself calm. "You don't know what you're doin' here. Maybe you better think on this."

She bristled. "Are you threatening me?"

"You ain't givin' me much choice."

"That's right," she said defiantly. "You have no choice. Get off my land."

"I can't do that. And I won't. I ain't leaving the Lazy C."

"You will leave today!"

"It ain't your decision to make, Miss Rosita."

"This is *my* spread!"

"Stocked with beef me and my men risked our lives gatherin'."

"You mean rustling."

"Have it your way. The results are the same." He smiled, somewhat coldly this time.

His casual defiance gave her pause. "You . . . will not do as I say?"

"No."

"Then I will get the law."

Slattery laughed shortly. "You mean Belcher?"

"Yes."

"You won't get much satisfaction from him."

She looked at him for a long moment, digesting this. He saw a despairing realization cross her face.

"You mean . . . you own him too?"

"Afraid so, Miss Rosita."

"Then I'll go to Jack French of the Bench. Dan Wilson of the Bar N. And Hendrik on the north range. They'll drive you and your gunslicks from this valley."

"If you do that, Miss Rosita, I will ruin you."

"You bluster, Slattery."

Very patiently, as if he were dealing with a slow-witted child. "Just consider a moment, Miss Rosita."

"Consider what?" she snapped.

"How easy it would be for someone to burn you out."

Her face went white. "What are you implying?"

"See, the big main house would go first," Slattery said. "Then the barns and all those big, fine horses you love to ride. Who knows? You might get caught up in the flames, running in there to save them. And when the smoke cleared, your stock would be gone—already halfway to market." He paused to let that sink in. "And no one would be the wiser, no one to mourn the passing of Rosita Calaveras—and her faithful retainer, Eduardo De Santos."

For the first time Rosita glimpsed a light in her foreman's eyes that truly frightened her. She was dealing with a predatory animal—not a man. But what truly dismayed her was how easily he had been able to conceal his rotting soul from her these past two years, and she shuddered anew at the realization that there had once been a time when she had actually considered marrying this man and presenting him with half ownership in the Lazy C.

47

"You son of a bitch," she hissed. "May you fry in hell!"

"Good," Slattery snapped. "Sounds like you know who you're dealin' with now. So why don't we forget this conversation, Miss Rosita? The Lazy C spread is the richest in this county, and you are on your way to becoming the most powerful cattlewoman in the territory. 'Stead of tryin' to cancel out what I've done to make the Lazy C what it is today, maybe you should think things over calmly—and then count your blessings."

"Count my blessings!" Rosita cried. "I have been sleeping with scorpions!"

"Soon enough, you'll be sleepin' with me, I'm thinkin'."

"You?"

"Don't deny it. I seen you lookin' at me once or twice. You got hot blood, and I'm just the man to take you down a peg."

She snatched up her riding crop and slashed Slattery across his cheek. Before she could strike him again, Slattery recoiled and pulled his horse back hastily. But unable to contain her fury at such filthy impertinence, Rosita spurred her black forward and continued to strike out at the cowering man, catching him with stinging effect about the head and shoulders.

Slattery took it for a while, even trying to laugh. But a tearing lash caught him across the nose—and a sudden explosive rage transformed him. Hunched over, he waited with a cold, deadly patience for the right moment, then grabbed the crop's stinging tip and pulled it out of Rosita's hand, flinging it away with a mean snarl.

Rosita wheeled her black and spurred away from him. But Slattery's blood was up now. He took after her, overtook her mount, and, reaching down, grabbed her bridle. Yanking back on it with cruel suddenness, he twisted the black's head and sent the horse plunging to the ground. With a tiny, startled cry Rosita went flying over its neck. She hit with sickening force and lay on her back, dazed.

Slattery flung himself from his mount, grabbed Rosita by the hair and hauled her brutally to her feet. She began to beat his chest. But to her dismay it only seemed to increase his strength. His fist still in her hair, he bent her head back and stepped close against her, aware that all this excitement had aroused him to a fever pitch. She saw both rage and lust blazing from his eyes as he chuckled meanly and thrust his erection hard against her.

Crying out, Rosita raked her fingers down the side of his face, catching the corner of one eye.

"Damn you!" he cried, flinging her to the ground.

As soon as she hit, he drew his Colt. Rosita read his expression with frightening accuracy. He had decided to kill her; he had no choice, since he knew she would never go along with his filthy schemes and would remain forever out of his reach.

She scrambled to her feet and began to run. He heard his heavy boots pounding after her. She changed direction like a terrified rabbit, but Slattery was too quick. Reaching out, he grabbed her shoulder and spun her around to face him.

"You don't like me, hey?"

She spat at him, catching him full in the face.

Holding nothing back, he clubbed her on the side of her head with the barrel of his revolver. Lights exploded deep inside her skull. She felt her knees turn to water and was barely sensible of the damp ground catching her limp body. Her eyes flickered open and she saw Slattery's face looming close, nightmarishly close. It was a mean, twisted mask of hate.

"Why don't you spit on me now, bitch?"

Unable to catch her breath, she could only stare up at him. Slattery straightened up and stepped back. She saw him level his revolver on her, then steady it as the front sight found her head. The Colt's yawning bore loomed as large as a cannon's mouth.

She closed her eyes. A moment before she lost consciousness, she heard the crack of a gunshot.

Chapter 5

Longarm had reined in his horse the moment he saw
the two figures struggling on the slope far below
him. He saw the woman wheel about and run from
her attacker, then watched in growing anger as the
man overtook her and slammed her to the ground
with a blow from his six-gun. When he saw the
man aiming down at the prostrate woman, Longarm
pointed his rifle skyward and sent a warning shot
into the air.

As the rifle's crack echoed across the long valley,
the man pulled back from the woman without firing
on her and shaded his eyes in an effort to catch
sight of Longarm's distant figure. Longarm cranked
and sent another round into the sky. This second
shot decided the man. He grabbed his horse's reins
and vaulted back into his saddle. Longarm urged
his mount to a full gallop and charged down the
long swale toward him. Throwing one futile shot
at Longarm, the man wheeled and rode off to the

west, heading toward a distant pass. He had disappeared by the time Longarm slipped from his saddle to kneel beside the unconscious woman.

She was lying face up, her magnificent crown of raven-black hair spilled over the grass. He leaned close and saw that she was breathing regularly. Above her left temple there was an oozing matt of snarled, bloodied hair where she had been struck. He shook her gently. Her eyelids flickered, then opened to reveal dark, molten eyes—as deep as the deepest pool. She stared up at him in confusion for a moment, then glanced fearfully around—for her assailant, he had no doubt.

"He's gone," he told her.

"Are you sure," she whispered, still looking fearfully about her.

"I'm sure. He's gone."

"Who was he?"

"Buck Slattery, my foreman."

She sat up slowly, her hand held up to her bloodied head.

"You took a pretty mean crack," he told her. "Better not try to move about just yet."

She started to nod in agreement, then caught herself as the sudden movement caused pain to rocket through her skull. "It feels like my head's cracked open," she said, managing a smile. "But what happened? I'm almost certain Slattery fired at me. I heard a shot . . ."

"That was me. I fired to distract him."

"You did?" She smiled wanly. "Then you saved my life. Thank you."

"Glad I came along when I did."

"Who are you?"

52

"Name's Long. Custis Long. And who might you be?"

"Rosita Cavaleras. I own the Lazy C."

"And you just fired your foreman."

"Yes."

"No wonder he was so angry."

"I just discovered he's an outlaw—worse, a rustler."

"I know. I saw him and his men rustle a trail herd some distance back in the mountains southwest of here."

"I've been such a fool. All this time he's been stocking Lazy C range with rustled cattle, and I was too stupid to realize it."

"You just found out what's he's been doing?"

"I know it sounds hard to believe."

He smiled at her. "I believe you. How far is your ranch from here?"

"Not far. Over that next line of hills."

"I'll ride over there and bring back a buggy for you. You can't stay on a horse in your condition. There's a chance you might have a concussion."

"Please. I'm sure I can ride."

"That's what you think now."

"Really, I can. Here, let me show you."

Longarm got to his feet, reached down to helped her up. But she disdained his helping hand and got quickly to her feet. The moment she was erect, however, she looked with sudden dismay at Longarm; then her face went chalk white and her knees buckled. Longarm stepped forward quickly and caught her in his arms, then lowered her gently back onto the ground. She clung to him a moment, muttering something about her head spinning off her shoulders.

After a moment, he asked, "You all right?"

"Maybe you better go get the buggy," she whispered.

Longarm gave her his Colt in the unlikely event Slattery returned to finish what he had started, then set out for the Lazy C. As he rode off, a horseman loomed in the pass to the west and watched him ride off in the direction of the Lazy C.

The Lazy C was an impressively prosperous ranch, Longarm noted as he rode through the big gate into the compound. The main house was palatial. Painted a gleaming white with a red, shingled roof, it was two stories high and boasted a balcony supported by four white columns which extended the full length of the house. Its veranda was wide and spacious. A blacksmith shop stood close by the bunkhouse. The horse barn was huge, the fences and corrals well-kept.

As he neared the main house, a Lazy C ranch hand stepped out of the bunkhouse, strapping on his gunbelt. He was joined by a black smithy toting a small crowbar. The two men started across the yard to intercept him. The smithy's face was streaked with soot, his powerful, bared torso shiny with perspiration. In his powerful hands, the crowbar looked no more substantial than a toothpick. An ancient cowpoke stepped out of the barn leading a bay. One look at Longarm and he sent the horse back into the barn with a sharp crack on its rump, then hurried over to join the other two, his only weapon a pitchfork he yanked from the ground. He looked as if he had been whittled from an old fence post.

Longarm halted his mount and waited for the

three men to reach him. When they did, he dismounted.

The one who had buckled on his gunbelt had the look of a typical hard case. His face was narrow and pinched, his eyes set close together. As he neared Longarm, he drew his six-gun.

"Who the hell are you, mister?"

"That don't matter right now."

"That so?" asked the smithy, his powerful voice menacingly quiet.

Longarm turned his head to address him. "That's right. What matters is the owner of the Lazy C."

The beat-up old wrangler stepped closer. "Talk straight, mister," he said. "What in blazes do you mean by that?"

"Your mistress has been hurt."

Concern sprang into the old man's eyes. "Miss Rosita? Hurt?"

"That's why I'm here. I've come for a buggy to bring her in."

"Whatta you mean hurt?" asked the gunslick. "Speak plain, mister. What happened?"

"Your foreman struck her down with his revolver. Hit her on the side of her head. She took such a mean crack she can't ride."

"Slattery did that?" the black asked. "Mister, you sure what you're sayin'?"

"I'm sure."

"I don't believe you," said the hard case.

"I saw Slattery do it myself. If I hadn't come by when I did, I believe he would have killed her."

The gunslick glanced around at the other two. "Hey, you can't believe this guy. He's loco. Slattery would never do such a fool thing!"

55

The blacksmith and the wrangler were obviously befuddled. What Longarm was telling them about their foreman was simply too much for them to accept without question. It called for a radical rethinking of their loyalties. Longarm understood their confusion—but at the same time he was losing his patience. Though it was highly unlikely, there was always the chance Slattery would return to Rosita in Longarm's absence to finish her off.

"Dammit," he said, impatiently. "Don't you men care about your mistress? I told you. She's been hurt and she's alone out there! Someone hitch up a wagon."

That was enough for the wrangler. Dropping the pitchfork, he turned and hustled back across the yard, heading for the barn. The blacksmith turned to Longarm.

"You want me to go with you?"

"I'd appreciate it."

"You got a name, mister?" the gunslick asked sullenly.

"Long. Custis Long."

"You mind tellin' me what you're doin' in these parts?"

"No. Don't mind at all. Just passin' through. Now how about holstering that sidearm? Don't seem very hospitable."

"I'll holster it when I'm good and ready."

"Put it away, Dimmy," said the blacksmith.

Dimmy gazed up at the black as if to challenge his right to tell him what to do—thought about it a moment, then grudgingly dropped his weapon back into its holster.

"I'm Ben Smith," the smithy said, looking back

at Longarm. "That's the name they gave me, anyway."

"Howdy, Ben."

The pound of hoofbeats sounded suddenly behind them. Longarm turned around to see Rosita astride her black, galloping through the ranch gate. The horse's reins were trailing and Rosita was hanging so low over the horse's neck that for a moment Longarm thought she was in immediate danger of falling off. But as the horse pounded closer, he saw Rosita's head and one fist buried in the stallion's thick mane. With Ben and the others, he hurried over to intercept her horse. As Longarm grabbed its trailing reins, it reared, causing the woman to tumble from the saddle. But Ben was ready for that and caught her in his arms.

Longarm let go of the reins and saw where his gun where had fallen to the ground from her hand. He picked it up, saw that one round had been fired, then holstered it. Meanwhile, Ben was holding the barely conscious woman as tenderly as if she were a bouquet of fresh-cut flowers.

"Take her into the house," Longarm told him.

By the time they got to it, an impassive Shoshone Indian woman as big and round as a barrel was waiting for them on the veranda. Ben carried Rosita up the veranda steps, Longarm right behind him. The Shoshone woman led the way into the big house and up the stairs to the second floor to Rosita's bedroom. Ben let her gently down onto her bed and stepped back.

The Shoshone woman leaned close to study the bloody tangle of hair over Rosita's temples, then hurried from the room. What she intended to do,

Longarm had no idea, but he was reasonably certain Rosita was in competent hands. He thanked Ben with a nod. The black man left the room. Longarm slumped into a cushioned rocker beside the bed, his eyes on Rosita. Unnaturally pale though her face was, it was still a countenance of breathtakingly loveliness, as fresh as the morning dew. It must have been her profound innocence, Longarm mused, that had enabled Slattery to take advantage of her so completely.

Rosita turned her head and opened her eyes. He leaned close.

"What happened?"

"He came back," she said, her hushed voice barely audible.

"Slattery?"

"Yes. I waited until he got close. Then I sat up and shot at him. I think I hit him."

"Then you got on your horse and rode in?"

"Yes. He started to follow me, then dropped off."

"Maybe you did hit him."

"But he was still able to ride."

"You did fine."

"I should have killed him. He was that close."

"Maybe so, but you're safe now. That was pretty fair riding."

"I don't even remember getting here."

"Well, you did. It was Ben caught you when you tumbled off your horse."

She closed her eyes then and relaxed. Some color had returned to her cheeks. The Shoshone woman returned with a pan of water and fresh towels folded over her arm. Rosita opened her eyes and smiled with relief at sight of her.

"Hello, Blossom."

The ghost of a smile crossed the woman's flat, impassive face, and, without a glance at Longarm, she set the pan down on the nightstand, dipped the towels into the water, and began placing cold compresses on Rosita's brow. Satisfied that all that could be done for Rosita was being done, Longarm left the room.

The three Lazy C hands were waiting for him in front of the veranda. The hard case spoke up first. "You got any proof what you said about Slattery?"

"You saw the condition Rosita was in. I told you what happened."

"All we saw was her ridin' in," the hard case said. "And you said she was hurt too bad to ride."

"Something spooked her."

"Yeah? What?"

"Slattery came back for her. She just told me."

"But we don't know that for sure now, do we. You could tell us anything—and we'd have to take your word."

"Then don't take my word. Wait for Rosita to come around. She'll tell you what happened."

"Yeah, Dimmy," Ben said. "We can wait and let Miss Rosita can tell us what happened."

"Shut up, nigger."

The big black's face showed no reaction as he sucked in his gut. But he gave no response to Dimmy's insolence. It was obvious he had already had plenty of practice taking this man's shit. But that didn't mean he liked it. Or that he wouldn't someday show just how he felt about it.

The wrangler took off his hat and ran his hand through a thatch of white hair. "Mister, you sayin' it was Slattery who did that to Miss Rosita?"

"That's what I said."

"Then, hell's fire," the old cowpoke said to Dimmy, "I sure ain't goin' to work for him."

"Sure. Go ahead," Dimmy said. "Throw away your meal ticket."

"Well, I don't care. I ain't working for him—not if he did that to Miss Rosita!"

Ignoring the irate wrangler, Dimmy drew his six-gun so smoothly it seemed almost to materialize in his grimy hand. Cocking it, he leveled the bore on Longarm's gut. His narrow, craggy face broke into a mean grin.

"Don't make no sudden moves, stranger."

"Hey, Dimmy," cried the shocked wrangler. "What're you doin'?"

"Can't you see? I'm covering this bastard."

"Why?"

"I say we keep him here, locked up until Slattery gets back. A good place would be over there in the barn's grain room. I say he's the one hurt Rosita. He was tryin' to rape her. Hell, we ought to string him up. And when Slattery gets back, maybe he'll do just that."

The black reached over almost casually and twisted the six-gun out of Dimmy's hand. Like taking candy from a baby.

"Ain't very hospitable, Dimmy," the big man said, "you drawing on a stranger like that."

Ben handed the gun to Longarm.

"Damn you, nigger!" Dimmy cried, massaging his right hand. "You near broke my gun hand!"

"Stop whinin'," Ben told him. "With a broke gun hand, you'll be a damn sight safer."

Longarm stepped closer to Dimmy and dropped the man's Colt back into his holster. Then, with two sharp raps to his chest, he shoved him a couple of feet back on his heels.

"Get on your horse and ride out," Longarm advised. "You know where to find Slattery. And when you do, tell him Luke Carson's dead."

"Luke?" Dimmy asked, frowning. "You say Luke's dead—?"

"That's what I said."

"Mister, who *are* you, anyway?"

"A man fast losin' his patience. Get on your horse and ride out. Tell Slattery we'll be waiting here for him."

Dimmy backed away a few more steps, then turned and hurried toward the horse barn, glancing back over his shoulder like a whipped cur—a dangerous whipped cur. As soon as he rode out a moment later, Longarm turned to the blacksmith.

"Ben, I want you and your companion here to gather up all the weapons you can find and lug them into the house, then make sure of their loads. When Slattery and his gunslicks return, we'll hold them off as long as we can. Remember. He's already tried to kill Rosita once. We can't let him get another chance."

"Don't worry," said Ben. "He won't get it."

"You got any more hands nearby?"

"The cook's gone to town for provisions," Ben said. "But he'll be back soon, and he's got a couple of men with him."

"You think they'll take our side in this?"

"They're loyal to Eduardo and Miss Rosita, not to Slattery."

"Eduardo?"

61

"He came from Texas with Rosita's father. When he died, he became like a father to Rosita. He would not harm her."

"Where is he now?"

"He rode out to meet Slattery this morning."

"Then he knows what Slattery's up to?"

Ben shrugged. "I don't know. Maybe. But even so, he wouldn't let any harm come to Rosita."

"Well then, we'll just have to wait and see which way the cards fall."

As the two men headed for the bunkhouse to gather up the weapons, Longarm, anxious to check on Rosita's condition, went back inside the big house.

Chapter 6

Slattery dismounted and approached his waiting riders. The men were no longer at work. They had long since hazed the last bunch of freshly branded stock into the upper canyons and draws and were now lazing about on the cool grass alongside one of the many snow-fed streams that watered the valley's lush grasslands. He looked for but couldn't find Eduardo, and that set off a little warning bell deep inside him.

He saw no campfire and that irritated him. He wanted some hot Irish coffee to settle his nerves. He had managed to staunch the flow of blood from the flesh wound Rosita had inflicted in his right side, but it still burned like hell, and the fact that he had let her catch him like that set him off every time he thought of it.

He was so preoccupied, he paid little attention to the coldly furious, white-faced Eduardo who rode in a little while after he did, dismounted, and started toward him.

"Slattery!" the old Mexican cried, his voice harsh.

Slattery turned, alerted by the tight fury in Eduardo's voice. "What is it?"

"I did not stay here as you say. I followed you."

"So you followed me. So what?"

"I saw you!"

"You saw me what?"

"You try to kill Rosita!"

"You're crazy, old man."

"I saw you, I said! Miss Rosita was on the ground. You rode up to her with your gun out! You were ready to fire down on her, but she fired first!"

The Lazy C riders were on their feet by this time, alerted by the anger in Eduardo's voice—and by the incredible accusation he was making. His words brought a low murmur from their ranks and they moved closer as Eduardo turned to them, his angry glance seeking out those riders he knew were more faithful to him than to Slattery.

"Listen, compadres!" he told them. "It is true what I say. Slattery would have killed Rosita, but she fire on him and drive him off."

The Mexicans who had followed Eduardo and Rosita's father all the way up from the Rio Grande were the riders Eduardo was addressing, and his words brought a sudden fury to their dark faces. One look at them and Slattery knew they were accepting without question what the old son of a bitch was telling them.

"Hey, now," he told these riders, "Eduardo's crazy. I don't know what he's talkin' about. His eyes been playin' tricks on him."

"Does this mean you can explain what Señor Eduardo jus' tell us?" one of the Mexicans asked.

"Sure, I can. No question."

"Then go ahead, explain it to them," Eduardo challenged, his voice quivering with indignation.

"What happened was Miss Rosita fell from her horse. When I rode up to see if she was hurt any, she got all panicky and rode off. I let her go when I saw how upset she was."

"She did not fire on you?"

"Now why would she do a crazy thing like that?"

The seven Mexicans looked to Eduardo then, to hear his refutation of Slattery's explanation. Eduardo simply walked up to Slattery and grabbing the man's shirt, yanked it out of his pants to reveal the blood-stained bandanna Slattery had wrapped about his flesh wound.

"See for yourself!" Eduardo told his men. "It ees the wound Miss Rosita inflict on thees man! He is a liar. She shoot him to save her life!"

That did it.

Those men loyal to Slattery moved quickly to back their foreman. They numbered nine in all, two more than the Mexicans, and for a moment both groups seemed ready to face off, but before any one could draw a weapon Slattery stepped between them.

"Hold it!" he cried. "Hold it! We can settle this peaceably, I tell you. No need for any gunplay."

Sullenly, warily, the two groups relaxed and stepped away from each other.

"Eduardo," Slattery said, "keep your men under rein, and me and my boys will ride out without drawin' on you. You got my word on that. All I want is your word you won't try to cross me."

"All right, Slattery. But you mus' understand, this ees not the end of the matter."

"Come on, boys," said Slattery. "Mount up!"

"Where we goin', Buck?" ond of his riders wanted to know.

"Into town, to Emerald's saloon, where we can rest up and irrigate our tonsils. How's that sound?"

His riders brightened immediately at the prospect and headed for the rope corral to get their horses. As they saddled up, the Mexican riders gathered around Eduardo, watching them warily, their hands resting lightly on their gun butts.

Slattery waited until Eduardo and his riders were strung out on their way back to the Lazy C before making his move. To kill a snake, stomp on its head, he was thinking, as he led his riders off the ridge at a hard gallop. Eduardo's men shouted a warning to Eduardo. The old fool turned his head to see Slattery and his men bearing down on him. Bending low over his mount's neck, he drew his six-gun and begun firing just as Slattery and his men opened up on him.

A bullet slammed into the horse's chest. It stumbled and went down. Eduardo hit the ground hard. He flipped over and lay flat on his back without moving. Slattery pounded past his prostrate figure, sent a couple of rounds into him, and kept on past at full gallop, his men trailing, ready to cut down any pursuing Mexicans. The Mexicans sent a few futile rounds after them, then gave up and turned back to see to their fallen leader.

Without a glance back at De Santos's disappearing riders, Slattery rode on toward the Lazy C, a savage elation building within him. His hand had been forced. So be it. For too long he had been

66

pussyfooting around Rosita, too damn careful even to fart. Well, the hell with her. No more kissing ass. There was no chance now of him marrying the lovely, inaccessible Rosita and taking over the Lazy C. legally as her husband.

So now he would just take it from her—husband or not.

With De Santos out of it, Slattery could ride into the Lazy C and finish off Rosita. Then he would buy up the outfit. With no more need to rustle cattle, he'd end his relationship with H. C. Billingsly and settle in with Emerald as a respected and prosperous stockman.

There was only one nagging uncertainty.

Who was that rifleman who <u>had</u> chased him off, then left his weapon with Rosita? It could not have been that stranger Em had warned him about. Luke Carson had already been sent to take him out. But suppose Luke had botched it?

It was an unsettling thought, but one he quickly stifled as he found himself imagining how Emerald would like being the wife of a big rancher. She was always telling him how much she hated running that saloon.

A horseman appeared on a ridge to the north. At the sight of Slattery and his men he turned his horse and galloped off the ridge toward them, waving his hat to slow them down. As he got closer, he began shouting. But he was too distant for Slattery to make out what he was shouting.

"Hey," said Hunnicut as the rider loomed closer. "That's Dimmy!"

By that time Slattery, too, had recognized the

rider. He pulled his mount to a halt as the rest of his men pulled up around him to wait for Dimmy to reach them.

No longer shouting, Dimmy pounded closer and at last pulled his lathered horse to a shambling halt beside Slattery. Dimmy's narrow face was flushed with excitement. Slattery chuckled, certain he knew what all the fuss was about. He was way ahead of the man.

"Relax," he told Dimmy. "No need to get your bowels in an uproar. I know all about it."

"No, you don't!"

"Sure, I do. You come to tell me Rosita's been hurt. Right?"

"Sure, she's hurt, all right. And you did it. You gave her a mean crack on the head."

"A little misunderstanding. It don't mean a thing. I'll explain it to her when we get back to the ranch."

"Boss, that's what I come to tell you! You can't!"

Slattery frowned. "Why not?"

"There's someone there—at the ranch, I mean—waiting for you. He's the one rode in and told us Rosita was hurt."

"He did what?"

"He was the one told us what you did to Rosita."

"He got a name?"

"He didn't say. But he told me to tell you something."

"What?"

"It's . . . about Luke Carson."

"What about Luke?

"He's dead. That's what this guy said, anyway."

Slattery did not doubt it. And this told him who that rider was who had fired on him, then left the

68

revolver with Rosita—the same son of a bitch Pete had lost his life trying to kill. And now the bastard had taken care of Pete's brother, too. Shit! This fellow Custis Long had as many lives as a cat.

Slattery considered the situation. He had been in tighter spots than this. No man had ever stopped him yet, and this big drink of water would be no different. All he needed was time to find out who the hell he was and figure a way to stop him.

"What about Rosita?" he asked Dimmy. "How bad is she hurt?"

"The Shoshone's takin' care of her. She ain't dead, that's for sure."

"And this fellow Long's taking over the ranch?"

"That's the way it looks." He grinned crookedly. "He's got Dan and Ben on his side, anyway. Two greaser hands and maybe the cook."

Slattery's force outnumbered them easily. But still he did not like the odds. He had intended to act fast—get to the ranch before those Mexicans rode in with De Santos's body and take over. A neat fait accompli. But he couldn't count on that now. If he got hung up by this Long and his men, he'd find himself with De Santos's riders at his back.

"All right, men!" Slattery cried. "It looks like we *are* heading for town, after all. I'm dry as a bone."

Not a single rider protested as Slattery turned his horse and headed for Horsehead.

Later that same day Eduardo arrived back at the Lazy C. He was a severely wounded man, and he slumped painfully in his saddle. As he and his men rode into the compound, they were all visibly relieved to see Rosita and Blossom sitting in wicker chairs on the veranda. Blossom had wrapped a damp towel about Rosita's head. Obviously still weak, Rosita did not get up when they rode toward the house—not until she saw Eduardo's condition, Then, frowning in sudden concern, she got to her feet and remained upright, leaning on the veranda's support post.

By the time the riders pulled up in front of the veranda, Longarm and Ben were already lifting the wounded man down from his saddle. In Ben's arms the old man was held as lightly as a child. Blossom waited for them in front of the door, then led them inside. A concerned Rosita followed. De Santos was carried into his bedroom behind the kitchen and let down gently onto his bed.

Longarm bent over the old campaigner and pulled off his vest, then peeled back his shirt. Both garments were heavy with blood. He saw at once where a bullet had entered the left side of Eduardo's chest and shattered one of his ribs, then glanced off, leaving an exit wound just under his armpit. Both entry and exit wounds were inflamed. There was another wound on his thigh, but this was only a minor flesh wound. Stepping back, Longarm realized that Eduardo would have to count himself a very lucky man.

Blossom entered the room with towels and a large pan of steaming hot water. Rolling up her sleeves, she shooed them all out of the room.

Outside the house a few moments later, it was the oldest Mexican, Antonio Vargas, who told them what had happened, starting from the moment Eduardo rode into the camp to accuse Slattery of attempting to murder Rosita. When he finished, Rosita thanked him and slumped back in her wicker chair to digest all this.

"So Eduardo is still loyal to me," she said to Longarm.

"Eduardo and seven of his riders. Things are looking up."

"I suppose. But all this treachery."

"This is a fine spread, Rosita. It is like honey drawing bears, I'm afraid."

"Not bears—monsters, killers."

Longarm could not disagree with her.

"And to think that Eduardo was a party to all this rustling," she said sadly, in the manner of a little girl who had just discovered there was no Santa Claus. "He knew all along and did nothing to warn me."

"I imagine Slattery sucked him in gradually, asking him to look the other way whenever Slattery brought in a few mavericks, and before he knew it, he was part of Slattery's operation. He had no wish to hurt you, I'm sure."

"He has been like a father to me."

"Then don't go too hard on him now. This is a good time to pay him back for all those years of caring. I'm sure he's punishing himself far more than you could."

She nodded. "Yes," she said. "I suppose you're right. But what do we do now? I told you what Slattery threatened. He wants to take this ranch from me, and he won't stop at burning me out if I refuse to let him. He's got enough men still loyal to him to do it—and that's not counting Sheriff Belcher."

"I've already met the sheriff. I don't think we have much to fear from that quarter."

"But don't you see, Longarm? Belcher is the only

71

law in these parts. All he has to do is look the other way and Slattery will have free rein to destroy me and any other spread that stands in his way."

"Then I suggest we look for allies."

"You mean the other ranchers in this valley?"

"Just give me a map of some kind, and I'll go visit each outfit personally."

"But they hate the Lazy C. And now that I know why, I don't blame them."

"It's a different poker deck we're dealing now. Slattery is no longer your foreman, and the Lazy C is no longer a haven for rustled cattle. The other cattlemen in the valley won't see the Lazy C as a threat any longer."

"But will they believe that?"

"There's one way they will for sure."

"What's that?"

"Offer to share your cattle with them, divide them evenly. You'll end up with a lot less cattle fattening on your ranges, but you'll still be in good shape— and so will the other spreads."

"Yes," she said eagerly, "that *would* be the thing to do, wouldn't it!"

"It would help a lot, Rosita. And give Slattery a lot less incentive to take over the Lazy C."

"When will you leave?"

"First thing in the morning. Slattery will be making his move before long, I figure, so we have to move fast."

"Who will you leave in charge while you're gone?"

Without bothering to consult him in the matter, Longarm realized, Rosita had made him the Lazy C's new ramrod. For a moment he considered protesting. Then he shrugged inwardly and decided to save any protests for later. With old De Santos out of action, Rosita sure as hell did need a foreman. It wouldn't hurt for him to take the job for a while, at least until he got his hands on Slattery again.

"I'll leave Vargas in charge," he said.

"Yes," she said, "that's a good choice. I've always liked Antonio, and he's a fine, hardworking hand."

"How's your head?"

"I haven't even thought about it since Eduardo rode in."

"You seem a lot stronger."

"I am."

"This man, Slattery. How well did you know him?"

"I knew very little about him. I much preferred the company of my horses."

"You didn't like him, then."

"No. But he did his job well, I thought, and Eduardo seemed satisfied."

"So that settled it for you."

"Yes." She smiled impishly at him. "You can hit me if you like; I was such a fool."

"Slattery already took care of that chore, I'm afraid."

"Yes," she said glumly. "So he did."

"Rosita, does Slattery have a scar?"

"Yes, he does."

"Where?"

"On the inside of his arm. It extends from his elbow clear to his wrist. Why do you ask?"

"Just curious is all."

She tipped her head and gazed at him for a moment. "Maybe now I'm getting to understand who you are and why you dropped out of the sky to save me. It's Slattery you're after, isn't it."

73

Longarm shrugged.

"Are you a lawman?"

"Do you see a badge on me?"

"That's no answer."

"It'll have to do, Rosita."

"For you, maybe, but not for me."

"Ever here that expression, 'Never look a gift horse in the mouth'?"

"Is that what you are, a gift horse?"

"Why not look at it that way?

Blossom appeared in the doorway.

Rosita got quickly to her feet. "How is Eduardo?"

"He sleep now. Come in for supper."

At that moment the cook rang the triangle for the Lazy C hands. Longarm had been eating in the bunkhouse with Ben and the other hands until now, more than pleased with the skills of the Lazy C's cook. But as he started down the porch steps on his way to the bunkhouse, Rosita reached out and took his hand.

"Longarm," she said, "eat inside with me tonight."

Offering no objection, Longarm followed Rosita into the house.

Chapter 7

Buck Slattery watched the sheriff slouch from the saloon. A weaving, barely coherent Dimmy stumbled out after him. Dimmy had tried to drink the sheriff under the table and failed. With such allies, Slattery realized, he should look for help. He glanced morosely around him, aware of the insistent ache in his side from that damned flesh wound.

His riders were crowding the Horsehead. It was near closing time, and most of them had a girl at their elbow, some more than one. This unexpected holiday from the Lazy C's routine bothered them not at all, and at times Slattery found himself wincing as their liquored-up voices cut through the saloon and their boisterous laughter boomed off the close walls.

Will pushed in through the batwings. When he spotted Slattery, he went straight for his table, hat in hand.

"What do you want, Will?" Slattery asked, knowing full well what the kid was after.

"Mr. Slattery, I just spoke to my old boss at the livery. He says he'll hire me back with a ten-dollar raise. He says he needs me."

"So you want to go back to shoveling horse manure."

The kid nodded.

"Well now, if shit kicking is your highest ambition in life, then I won't stand in your way."

"Thanks, Mr. Slattery."

"Just one thing."

The kid waited nervously.

"Don't you let on a word about what you saw up in them hills. And remember, you were a part of it." He smiled coldly. "You might say every cow you branded has your name on it."

"I won't say a word to no one," the kid promised eagerly. "Honest, Mr. Slattery."

"All right. Get out of here."

The kid clapped his hat back on and almost ran from the saloon.

"What was that all about?" asked Emerald as she approached his table.

He waited until she sat down before replying.

"I just released Will Hammer from the threat of eternal damnation."

"So he's back shoveling shit."

Slattery nodded. Emerald waved to the barkeep for drinks, then placed her hand on Slattery's forearm.

"I know you got trouble all of a sudden, Buck. But after all this time, I really am glad to see you."

Slattery smiled crookedly at her. "Every cloud has a silver lining, eh?" He patted her hand, then leaned back in his chair, an intent frown on his face. "The thing is, I got to move fast if I don't want to lose it all—everything I been building these two years." He shook his head and blew out his cheeks. "Did you get a good look at this fellow Long?"

"I was sitting at this table with him."

"Well, what can you tell me?"

"I think you got a wildcat by the tail. Or maybe a panther, by the look of him. He's over six feet with gunmetal blue eyes and a longhorn mustache he takes good care of. He moves spooky fast for anyone that large. He threw Belcher down them stairs out back of Irene's even though the sheriff had his gun in his back. Belcher is still sore."

"Too bad he didn't break his neck."

"From the way he squealed, you'd think he had."

The barkeep set down a shot of Scotch, neat, in front of Emerald and placed a fresh stein of beer before Slattery. Emerald swept up the shot glass, threw the whiskey down her throat, blinked, and smiled at Slattery. Wondering, as always, how the hell she could do that without a chaser, he hauled his beer closer and drank deep.

"You say Long told you he was on the run?"

Emerald nodded. "When I questioned it, said he didn't look like a man on the owl hoot trail, he laughed it off. I don't believe him, Buck. I swear he's a lawman."

"Well, he don't act like one—assaulting a sheriff."

"Now, Buck, you don't really think of that lumbering fart as a lawman, do you? Just because we got him elected sheriff and pinned a tin badge on his vest."

Slattery grinned back at her. "He sure don't inspire

much confidence in his abilities."

"What he inspires is ridicule."

Slattery shook his head in frustration. "This guy Long should be dead by now. Pete had him out in front of that herd, leading him with his hands buckled to his saddle horn. But the bastard got out of it somehow. I just wish to hell I knew what his game is."

"Maybe it's to drive you crazy."

"Or worse."

"So what are you going to do about him?"

"That's what I'm tryin' to figure. Right now Long is probably holed up at the Lazy C with Rosita and them Mexicans."

"What about De Santos?"

"If he ain't dead, he's sure as hell out of action. Right now, the only thing standin' between me and the Lazy C is Rosita and this stranger. That means I'll just have to go out there and take them."

"You make it sound easy."

"Hell, Em, I know it ain't. But I don't know any other way to handle this."

"I know another way."

"I'm listenin'."

"Pull out."

He looked at her in surprise. "Pull out?"

"Yes."

"After all the time I put into this?"

"Buck, forget the Lazy C. I got enough—more than enough—saved up for the both of us. We could go to San Francisco. I could open up a parlor house there."

"You mean live off you?"

"And my girls."

78

He shook his head emphatically. "I ain't goin' to let no woman take care of me, Em. No woman and especially no girls."

"Too proud?"

"Sure I am, and if I weren't, you wouldn't have nothin' to do with me."

Emerald had no response to that, but he could see she agreed with him.

"Well, if you're goin' to stay here and take back the Lazy C, maybe you better watch out for them other ranchers."

"What d'you mean?"

"Suppose they join up with the Lazy C to take you on?"

Slattery frowned. "I suppose they could do that. Don't seem likely, though. But if they *did* join forces with Long, the fat *would* be in the fire."

Slattery's mind was racing now. He wasn't worried about Nils Hendrik's Bar H. Hendrik was one of the meanest, filthiest men he'd ever come across—and the most dangerous. Dimmy seemed to get along with Hendrik just fine, but Slattery didn't trust him. Luckily, no one else in the valley did, either. So he could forget about the Bar H. But the Bench and Dan Wilson's Bar N were different. Which meant he had to find a way to discourage Wilson and French from that any alliance with the Lazy C.

Slattery had an inspiration. He grinned at Em.

"Now what?" she asked warily.

"I have a way to keep them other spreads from joining up with the Lazy C."

"How?"

"Simple. I'll close the town to them if they do. Without supplies, they'll dry up."

"Can you do that?"

"I own the sheriff. He's the law in this town, ain't he? And Potter and Phillips will do as I say. No question about that."

Potter ran the only mill in town and Phillips the general store. Both men were fugitives from justice—Potter for embezzlement, Phillips for a swindling scheme that had gone awry. It was Slattery who had brought them here and bankrolled them. Under the circumstances, he would have no trouble at all convincing Potter and Phillips to squeeze out the ranchers if it came to that.

"That's a pretty mean trick."

"Ain't it though?"

"It might come to gunfire."

"It probably will if the outfits ride in here demanding supplies and provisions and feed for their saddle horses—and don't get any. No question. But I've got plenty of men in town here with nothing better to do but practice up on their shooting."

"And their drinking."

Slattery glanced around at his roistering men. "Yeah, well, I'll be riding out against the Lazy C first chance I get."

"You know, it might work."

"It will," Slattery said. "I'm sure of it."

He leaned back in his chair and reached out for his beer. Despite the nagging ache in his side, he was beginning to feel a lot better. He never liked to deal himself into a game unless he had an ace up his sleeve. Tomorrow he would visit Potter and Phillips, and then he'd send Will Hammer out with a note to the Bench and the Bar N.

Then he would have his ace.

He finished his beer and wiped his mouth with the back of his hand, then glanced at Em. It had been a long day and he was ready for his reward. She caught the look in his eyes and lifted her eyebrows questioningly.

"That's right, Em," he said, grinning. "Looks like its time for you and me to go upstairs."

"You're a real poet, you are. How could any woman resist?"

He scraped his chair back and stood up, grinning. "The poetry will come later. Right now we got other business."

Her green eyes gleaming, she stood up and preceded him across the saloon floor, heading for the stairs that led to her second floor apartment.

A few moments earlier, on his way past the restaurant, Dimmy pulled up woozily and clung to the wall to prevent himself from crashing to the boardwalk. Glancing through the restaurant window, he saw that pig Irene placing a platter down before a late customer.

It occurred to him then that Long had been upstairs in Irene's bedroom when he gunned down Luke. She had always been too good for Dimmy, but not too good for that bastard Long. Thinking of Irene sleeping with Luke's killer caused Dimmy to work himself into a seething fury. It was all he could do to keep himself from barging into the restaurant and beating the hell out of that fat blond bitch.

No. There was a better way.

He lurched into the alley beside the restaurant. Stumbling more than once in the pitch darkness, he came out behind the restaurant and found the steps leading up to Irene's apartment. He climbed them, found Irene's door locked, and kicked it open. Inside, when he caught sight of Irene's sofa, he staggered over to it. He collapsed facedown on the soft cushions and felt himself spinning off into oblivion. . . .

Longarm sat up in bed. Rosita, wearing a long, pale nightdress, floated cloudlike across the room to him. Her dark hair was combed out, and as she paused beside his bed and leaned over him the fragrance from her long tresses caused his groin to tighten involuntarily.

"Are you awake, Custis?" Rosita whispered.

"I'm awake. Wide awake."

Her teeth gleamed as she smiled.

"Blossom said I should join you."

"Nice of her to be so thoughtful."

"She . . . she said it was time I knew a man. That's why I insisted you sleep in the house tonight."

"You mean this is your first go at it?"

"Yes. For a while I toyed with the idea of allowing Buck Slattery to visit with me, but I could not bring myself to do it. Blossom did not like him, either. I'm so glad I waited. Blossom said you are twice the man Buck is. She says she likes your shoulders. And your eyes. She says they look straight at a person and do not shift away like men possessed by the devil."

"Nice to have such an endorsement."

She sat down on the bed beside him and leaned close, her dark tresses covering him, their sweet perfume clouding his senses, her dark eyes gleaming softly as she gazed deep into his.

"I think Blossom is right," she murmured, the

perfume of her breath searing him. "And I think you should take me."

"Take you?"

"Yes. Now."

"Just slow down a mite, will you?"

"You do not want me?"

"That ain't the point."

"What do you mean?"

"I mean it ain't me we got to worry about. It's you."

"Me?"

"You're a virgin, ain't you?"

"Of course."

"Well, that's quite a . . . responsibility for a man, and I don't think I should be the one—if you know what I mean."

"You think I should wait for my wedding night."

"Yes, I do."

"Well, I don't!"

"For goodness sake, Rosita, why not?"

"Custis, do you have any idea how long I'll have to wait for someone to show up and marry me? In these mountains, so far from civilization? I might even die an old maid."

"I don't think that's likely, Rosita."

"I certainly hope not." She took his hand in hers and leaned closer, their faces almost touching. "But I've been watching my horses breed for many springs now, and I must admit it—their wild, sometimes savage coupling has not left me unmoved—or without a desire to experience what they experience. Sometimes this . . . desire leaves me weak. Can you understand that?"

"Sure. I'm no dolt, not entirely."

"Then take me! What are you waiting for?"

"What about your head injury?"

"My head is fine now."

She shook her hair back off her shoulders and stood up in front of him, waiting.

"Well?"

He encircled her slim waist, pulled her close and kissed her, gently at first, then more probingly. At first she did not know what to do. Then her lips parted deliciously and with a sigh she opened to him. A small voice deep inside him told him to go slow, no matter how ready she might appear to be.

Drawing her onto the bed beside him, he gently disrobed her, then held her close, his lips moving lightly over her body. Everywhere. Behind her ears. On the nape of her neck. And finally her nipples, erect now, as rigid as bullets. She began to flow under him, moaning softly, uttering tiny, impatient cries.

"Custis!" she cried. "Now! I am ready! I tell you, I am ready."

He paid no heed as his lips found her thighs, the soft mound of her pubis, and explored further.

She began to thrust, her hands buried in his hair, her head twisting from side to side. She was beside herself. Every nerve in her body wanted completion, but Longarm had to be sure she was ready. She grew moist, and he left her pubis and moved up onto her belly, kissing it softly, then feasting on her high, soaring breasts, his tongue flicking at each erect nipple with devilish efficiency. Her fists began to beat on his back as she heaved wildly under him.

"Damn you," she cried. "I've seen my stallion mount his mare! You know what I want!"

She reached down and closed her fist about his erection.

"This!" she panted, attempting to scoot under him.

He pulled away playfully and kissed her neck, chuckling. Her teeth closed about his earlobe with such ferocity he almost cried out.

It was what he had been waiting for. He would not hurt her now. If he did, she would not mind. She was ready and so was he. Swiftly, he pulled her under him and thrust his knees between her thighs. Reaching down, he guided himself into her moist warmth, then plunged into her.

She cried out, more a yelp than a cry. He plunged deep again. This time she uttered a soft, delighted gasp.

"Oh, my God!" she cried, flinging her arms around his neck. "My stallion! You just severed me!"

He laughed and kissed her on the lips. "It only feels that way. You'll be as good as new in the morning."

"Better!" she cried.

"Lay still. That was just the opener."

Unable to hold back any longer, he began to heave roughly into her, swiftly picking up the tempo as she came alive under him and began matching him thrust for thrust, clumsily at first, but rapidly getting the hang of it. She began to pant; her arms tightened about his back. As he swept to and beyond his climax, he felt his warm seed spill into her.

Her eyes grew wide with astonishment.

"Is that it? Is that all?"

He leaned close and kissed her trembling eyelids. "No, that's not all there is."

"But . . ."

"Wait. Be patient."

He made no effort to pull out, but continued to smile down at her and kiss her about the face and body, waiting for himself to come alive again. It was not long before the incandescent warmth of her body enabled him to regain his erection. Her eyes grew wide as she felt him grow inside her. She hugged him still more tightly. This time, as he began to thrust gently, he placed his big hands under her buttocks and guided her thrusts. She caught his intent at once and cooperated beautifully. Her face began to flush. She laughed low, seductively.

"Yes," she whispered. "Oh, yes, I can feel it now! This time I'm the one can't stop."

He brought her along carefully, then found himself once again caught up as well. Soon, they were thrusting in unison, building nicely as they became truly the two-backed beast, locked together like pieces of a jigsaw puzzle. This time, a second before he did, she climaxed and uttered a high, exultant cry.

He came a moment later and sagged off her, laughing.

"There!" he said, smiling at her. "After that bugle call, I'm sure Blossom knows now that things have gone well."

"If she doesn't, I'll tell her myself."

"Just tell me one thing."

"Anything," she said, resting her head onto his chest.

"Why do you call her Blossom?"

Rosita laughed softly. "When she first appeared on our ranch, all she had was a potato sack for a dress and a fistful of wild flowers."

86

"Oh."

"Now, let's do that again."

"You really like it, huh?"

"Of course."

"So you want to get it right, that it?"

"Yes, hurry!"

Her hand snaked down to his crotch.

"Oh, my!"

"What?"

"It's not big anymore."

"Rosita," he said softly, "I think it is time for me to tell you about the birds and the bees. And men and women, too."

"Will that make you big again?"

"That depends."

"On what?"

"On how well you listen."

She snuggled still closer, and Longarm began to tell her of the first woman he ever had. It was on a hot summer afternoon in a hayloft back in West-by-God-Virginia. This first young lady's needs had been direct and uncomplicated, which left it to the other women he explored thereafter to refine his expertise.

Though Rosita's eagerness to hear his exploits kept her alert at first, she was soon fast asleep in his arms. Without having to reveal to Rosita that he was only a man—not a superman—Longarm dropped off himself, his arms still around her, the perfume of her body the last thing he remembered.

Chapter 8

By mid morning one of the many streams that coiled through the valley meandered away from Longarm and lost itself in the gently rolling parkland. Sorry to lose the stream's melodious company, Longarm stayed on the rutted trace he had been following since early that morning. An hour later he pulled to a halt on a rise that gave him a clear view of Dan Wilson's Bar N Ranch.

He nudged his mount off the ridge and after about fifteen more minutes reached the Bar N and rode in through the gate. Shaded by a thick clump of cottonwoods, the main house was constructed solidly of logs, the bunkhouse and cookshack of rough, unplaned lumber. The blacksmith shop was an open, three-sided affair with a rusting tin roof. A well-kept network of pole corrals behind the two barns opened onto the horse pasture. The Bar N struck Longarm as a solid, well-run outfit.

Before he reached the gate Longarm had seen ranch hands lining up in front of the hitch rack before the main house. They were carrying rifles, and now as he crossed the compound on his way to the house, they left the hitch rack and strode toward him, their faces grim with purpose. From the house emerged Dan Wilson, the Bar N's owner, and his wife, Samantha.

Longarm had not expected a warm welcome.

Wilson had had a running feud with the Lazy C for years now. As Rosita explained it, the trouble had something to do with a boundary dispute near a stream bordering their land, and some timber rights in the hills back of Lazy C. Rosita apologized for not being able to tell Longarm much more than that.

He pulled his horse to a halt, waiting for the usual invitation to light. But it did not come. What he saw on Wilson's lean face was, at best, a grim determination to have as little as possible to do with Longarm or the Lazy C. Though it was not good manners to talk to someone on foot while still in the saddle, Longarm decided he had no other course open to him.

"Howdy, ma'am," he said, touching his hat brim in salute to Wilson's wife.

She mumbled a response, then glanced at her husband.

"Who are you, mister?"

"Name's Custis Long."

"And you're riding for the Lazy C, I understand."

"That's right. I rode over to have a talk with you— a peaceable talk, that is. Mind if I light and set a spell?"

"You can light if you want, Long," Wilson replied coldly.

Longarm swung off his horse and dropped its reins over the hitch rack and ascended the porch steps. Mrs. Wilson opened the door and led him into the house. Wilson followed in behind Longarm and closed the door after them.

They came to a halt in the kitchen. Longarm was impressed. Most of the furniture was handmade, including the plank table. But everything was superbly cared for and as clean and fresh as a spring morning. There was not a speck of dust on the floor or on any of the chairs and tables. The dishes, standing face-out in the open cupboard, positively gleamed.

Wilson sat down at the table and Longarm took a seat across from him. On a huge black wood stove sat a pot of freshly brewed coffee. From this Samantha poured their coffee. She placed a pitcher of heavy cream and a jar of honey down in the center of the table, sat down next to her husband, looked at Longarm, and waited. But it was Wilson who spoke first.

"I know why you're here, Long."

"That right?" Longarm put down the cream pitcher.

"You want the Bar N to throw in with the Lazy C."

"That's why I rode over here, all right. You mind telling me how you knew that?"

"We heard," Wilson said. "That's all you need to know."

"All right, Wilson," Longarm said, "Rosita told me you've been having trouble with the Lazy C. So I can understand how you feel. But Buck Slattery was behind that rustling and he's not Lazy C's ramrod any more. So I'm here to see if we can't let bygones be bygones and work together."

"So you can take on Buck Slattery and his imported guns."

"Can you think of a better course of action? Don't tell me you admire Buck Slattery and all he's done for this valley."

Wilson glanced at his wife. Something very subtle passed between them.

"All right," Wilson said, seemingly relieved. "No sense in holding this back. I got a message from Buck Slattery this morning, hand-delivered. It was a warning. We help you and we'll be locked out of Horsehead. That means no mash, no grain, and no provisions like salt, flour, potatoes. You can see what that would do to us."

"He can do that? Close off the town completely?"

"He owns the sheriff and everyone else in that town. Yes, he can do that."

"Then this is why you won't help the Lazy C."

"That's one pretty good reason. Why should we stick our neck out for an outfit that never made any effort to treat us right, whose ramrod for the past two years has been intercepting our trail herds?"

"I told you. That's all behind us now. You might say the Lazy C's under new management. It was Slattery who's been rustling your cattle, not Rosita. She knew nothing about it."

"That Mex knew."

"I admit that. De Santos knew. And right now he's lying on his bed with a bad gunshot wound because he finally turned on Slattery. Look, Wilson, alone you have no chance against Slattery. But you won't be alone if you throw in with us."

"Sure. Sure. Hang together or we'll all hang separately. But how do I know the other ranchers will join us? They got no reason to. They could lose as much as us if Slattery closes the town to them."

"But you ranchers can't just sit back and let Slattery bully you like this."

Wilson shook his head wearily. "If you want my advice, Long, you'll get out of this while you can. And if you've taken such a fancy to Rosita Calaveras, take her with you."

"And Slattery will take over the Lazy C again. Do you really think you can live with that?"

"All Slattery wants is the outfit. Once he gets that, he'll cut out the rustling. He'll be one of us then. It'll all be different."

"And you really believe that, do you?"

Wilson's face went beet red and for a moment Longarm thought the man might empty his coffee cup in his face. "Who the hell are you to question me, Long?" Wilson said. "Where'd you come from, anyway? For all I know, you might be just one more drifter runnin' from the law. Once you get rid of Buck Slattery and take over the Lazy C, you might turn into another Slattery."

"Not possible."

"Prove it."

"Rosita is offering to give back the cattle you've lost these past years as a result of Slattery's rustling. Of course, she can't give you an exact acounting, and she'd have to divide the Lazy C stock evenly among the other ranchers. But she'd do her best to even things up."

Samantha looked at her husband. "Why, Dan," she said. "That certainly is fair, don't you think?"

Wilson pursed his lips and sat back in his chair, studying Longarm's face—as if he could divine in his countenance the veracity of Rosita's offer.

"Well?" Longarm prompted.

"I'd like to believe you, Long. But I ain't never heard of anyone doin' a thing like that."

"And you won't ever again."

Samantha was about to say something, but a sharp glance from Wilson silenced her. Looking back at Longarm, he shook his head emphatically.

"I can't chance it, Long. I can't go against Buck Slattery and his gunslicks. It's too risky. I don't want no trouble. All I want is to be left alone."

Longarm took a deep breath. He had pulled out all the stops. But nothing, it seemed, could break through this man's fear of Slattery. Before Longarm could say any more, Wilson pushed back his chair and stood up.

"You caught me in the middle of a busy day, Long. There's a lot of work yet to be done before sundown. I'm sure you understand."

Longarm finished his coffee and got to his feet, then strode from the kitchen. Outside by the hitch rack, he turned for a moment to nod his farewell to the Wilsons, then vaulted into his saddle, wheeled his mount and rode from the compound. He was anxious to reach Jack French's outfit by midafternoon at the latest.

Not that he gave himself much hope after this turndown. He now understood why Slattery's tactics had been so successful in this valley: the quality of his opposition. It was funny how people who wanted no trouble, who just wanted to be left alone, inevitably found themselves with more trouble than they could ever handle.

94

They didn't see how their fear of trouble only invited it.

Jack French, the owner of the Bench, was waiting for Longarm astride a big chestnut on a rise overlooking his ranch. Which meant that the same messenger who had ridden out to Dan Wilson's Bar N had visited Jack French as well.

Five ranch hands sat on their mounts behind him. French was a bear of a man. Clean-shaven, with a square chin and a powerful blade of a nose, he looked to be in his mid-thirties. As Longarm rode closer, French put his horse down the slope, his riders trailing behind him.

"Who're you, mister," he asked as he pulled to a halt alongside Longarm, "and what're you doin' on Bench land?"

"Name's Long, and I figure you already know what I'm doing here."

"I got a pretty good idea. You're from the Lazy C."

Longarm looked around and spotted a clump of birch on a knoll not too distant. "Maybe we could ride over to them birches," he suggested. "Climb off these hot saddles and have a little talk. It'd be a damn sight cooler over there."

"I didn't ride out here to talk."

"Then why did you?"

"To order you off my land."

"Why're you being so hard to deal with? You look like a reasonable man. Why not hear me out?"

French hesitated a moment, then bit. "All right. What've you got to say?"

Longarm turned his horse and booted him up the knoll toward the birches. When he reached their

95

shade, he dismounted and looked back. A grumbling Jack French was riding up the knoll after him. French's riders remained where they were. Longarm slumped down onto the cool, fragrant grass, leaned his back against one of the birch's tree trunks, and took out two cheroots. When French dismounted and approached him, Longarm offered him one.

A moment later French was sitting on the grass beside Longarm, puffing on his cheroot. His dark eyes were still wary, however, as he waited for Longarm to tell him what he wanted.

"I'm curious, French. How'd you know I'd be ridin' out here today?"

"Didn't. Five miles back when you forded the Little Rock stream, one of my men spotted you. I just put two and two together."

"I understand you just got a message from Buck Slattery."

"That's right. Will, the kid works at the livery stable, brought it later this morning."

"And Slattery's threatening to freeze you out of Horsehead if your outfit throws in with the Lazy C. That right?"

French nodded."

"Well, listen to this, French. Rosita's willing to give back all the livestock Slattery's been taking. She'll divide her herds up evenly with the rest of the ranchers in this valley."

French's eyebrows shot up in appreciation of the offer. It was obvious he was impressed. For a long moment he studied the glowing end of his cheroot.

"And all we'd have to do is stop Buck Slattery," he said. "That it?"

"That's it."

"I suppose it don't sound so difficult to you, mister—but it ain't as easy as all that. Buck Slattery owns this valley. That's the long and the short of it. If his men keep me out of Horsehead, I won't get any provisions and, mister, I have need of provisions. And another thing. The Lazy C has never done a thing for me. So why should I help it now that Buck Slattery's about to take it over completely?"

"It makes no difference to you that Slattery's been stealing you blind?"

French smiled. "Two can play at that game, mister. I've taken in a few mavericks myself, most of them Lazy C strays. That fool Slattery's so busy robbing everyone else, he never even noticed."

"You won't complain then if things remain the same?"

"They always do, Long. Nothing changes. Not really. Though sometimes things do manage to get worse."

"French, what about Rosita Calaveras?"

"What about her?"

"Don't you care what happens to her? You're willing to see Slattery take her land from her and drive her out of this valley?"

For the first time Longarm got a real reaction, a sudden breakthrough of genuine feeling. "What do you mean I don't care?" French exploded. "I didn't say that."

"Well, if you care—help her."

"Dammit, why should I help her? She's been livin' in that big fancy house with Buck Slattery for the last two years. She's nothin' but a two-bit whore."

"You're wrong, French."

"So *you* say."

"I mean it. She was more interested in breeding saddle horses than bedding Slattery. Fact is, she couldn't stand the man. And De Santos was there to keep them both decent."

"You believe that?"

"I know it."

"You just rode into this valley. What do you know?"

"French, can you tell a genuine coin from a counterfeit."

"Of course I can."

"Well, so can I. And I'm telling you Rosita never let that son of a bitch near her."

"I'd like to believe that."

"Then believe it."

"Aw, hell, Long. Even if what you're saying is true, that don't change anything."

There was a hint of pain in French's voice, the sad awareness of something irretrievably lost. And Longarm knew what that was, his deep and abiding concern for Rosita. More than likely, he was in love with her. But his conviction that she had been sleeping with her foreman had torn him up inside, and there seemed no way now for him to think of her as he wanted to.

Sensing French's dilemma, Longarm said, "Why not give Rosita the benefit of the doubt, French? You might be doing both of you a favor. And one thing more. If you think Rosita is going to turn tail and run, you really *don't* know the woman."

Longarm flicked away the stump of his cheroot and and stood up, walked over to his horse, and swung into his saddle. With a quick wave, he rode down off the knoll, hoping to reach Nils Hendrik's Bar H before sundown.

A bald ridge overlooked the Bar H's ranch buildings. At its base, a mountain stream fed a thick stand of cottonwoods. In among the cottonwoods lay the careless scatter of the Bar H's buildings. What Longarm glimpsed through the trees as he rode closer was a single-story log cabin and a low sod-roofed bunkhouse overgrown with weeds, pole sheds, and a corral.

In the gathering twilight, a hapless air of neglect hung over the place. The low porch in front of the cabin was missing a few boards, and in the front yard a buggy with three of its wheels sagged miserably. On its side lay a grindstone, its shaft rusting. Old tree stumps pocked the front yard.

Longarm had almost reached the cabin when a man he assumed to be Nils Hendrik stepped through the doorway, a rifle cradled in his arms. A gaunt, unshaven man in his mid-forties with sky-blue eyes, a tangle of yellow, uncombed hair and a raw, sun-blasted face, he was barefoot and shirtless, and his trousers were held up by yellow braces. He had the slack, hollow-eyed look of a man who drank too many of his meals.

"Now who the hell might you be?" he asked Longarm.

Longarm pulled up, surprised. "You mean you don't know?"

Hendrik revealed a few yellow teeth in what passed for a grin. "No, mister, I don't know. And I don't much care. But if you don't tell me what you're doin' on my land, I'm liable to blow your fool head off, ridin' in here without no hail to the house. This here's Bar H land and it's mine."

"I'm Custis Long. And I'm from the Lazy C."

Hendrik expectorated a long rope of tobacco juice that splattered to the ground inches from the left front foot of Longarm's mount. "Yeah. That much I heard, you bootin' Slattery out of the Lazy C, but that don't mean nothin' to me. What're you doin' in my front yard?"

"I want to talk to you."

"That so?"

"About the Lazy C. Miss Rosita thinks it might be a good idea if your spread and the Lazy C linked up."

"Me link up with the Lazy C? Why?"

"To stop Buck Slattery."

"That's a tall order, mister." He grinned knowingly and leaned forward, his blue eyes bright with malice. "Tell me. Any other outfits in this valley joinin' up with her?"

"That's not the point, Hendrik."

"Sure it is."

"Hear me out. The Lazy C is willing to make a deal with any rancher that sides her in this."

"What kind of deal?"

"She will make amends for the cattle Slattery has rustled. Divide her herds among the valley's outfits."

"You mean give back what she took?" The idea obviously seemed ludicrous to Hendrik.

"That's what I said."

"Well, now—ain't that somethin'."

The man cocked his head as if he were seriously considering the proposal and Longarm knew then that Slattery had not sent any warning to Hendrik, threatening to freeze him out of Horsehead if he lined up with the Lazy C. This had to mean that Slattery knew Hendrik well enough to know it was highly unlikely Hendrik would join forces with the Lazy C.

Longarm was saddle sore and his horse needed a rest, so without waiting for an invitation from Hendrik, he dismounted and led his mount over to what remained of the hitch rack in front of the cabin.

"Thought I might light and set a spell," he told Hendrik.

"Yeah," Hendrik said, lowering his rifle, "maybe you better come inside and tell me more about this crazy deal you're offerin'."

Longarm dropped his reins over the hitch rack and followed Hendrik into his cabin. And immediately wished he'd stayed on his horse. The cabin's interior was smoky and close, the fetid air assaulting his nostrils with an awesome stench compounded of rotting garbage, rancid meat, unwashed underwear, and the awful stink of an unclean human.

The stove was thundering with a fresh load of kindling, and on it a battered coffeepot was spouting steam. The sink was piled high with dishes. Potatoes were spilling out of a torn sack in one corner. A sack of flour beside it had white footprints radiating from it out into the kitchen. Wherever Longarm's eyes lit he found litter. He had the sickening sense that he had stumbled into the lair of some wild animal—then corrected himself. No animal could live in such filth. Only the human animal was capable of fouling his own nest in this manner.

Ignoring the steaming coffeepot, Hendrik leaned his rifle against the table and lifted an earthen brown jug up onto the table. He set two tin cups down on the table and filled both. Longarm picked up his cup and tossed down the moonshine. It tasted like lit kerosene, blasting a hole in his stomach and filling his blood with fire.

Hendrik tossed his drink down as if it were a cup of spring water, then refilled Longarm's empty cup.

"Drink up," he said, grinning at Longarm.

Through watery eyes, his brain on fire, Longarm lifted the cup and managed to toss down his second dose of moonshine. It left him woozy, but to his relief, it dulled his sense of smell. He cleared his throat, held out his cup for another refill, then asked Hendrik if he was willing to consider seriously Rosita's deal.

Hendrik wiped off his mouth with the back of forearm. "If you think you can stop Buck Slattery, good luck to you, mister. How many riders you got backing you?"

"Ten, maybe."

"That's not enough."

"How large a crew do you have?"

"You're lookin' at it." He grinned.

Longarm was not surprised. But he was discouraged. His search for allies to help save the Lazy C was not going very well.

Without much enthusiasm, Longarm asked, "Well, then, will you join us?"

"Why don't you let me drink on it?"

Longarm watched Hendrik down another cup. It was remarkable. The moonshine appeared to have absolutely no effect on Hendrik, except perhaps to make his eyes a bit brighter.

Longarm pushed himself to his feet and stood in front of the table, swaying slightly.

"Guess I'll be ridin' back," he managed.

"What's the hurry, Long? Don't you want to stay here and convince me to join up with that Mexican whore?"

Longarm narrowed his eyes and stared at Hendrik, wondering why the man was suddenly trying to antagonize him.

"What're you up to, Hendrik?"

"I'm tryin' to get your goat, you goddamn asshole."

The moonshine was hitting Longarm now—hard. He turned and started blindly for the door. It had suddenly became absolutely imperative that he escape this cabin's gut-wrenching stench. He was almost to the door when it opened and he found the doorway blocked by Dimmy. There was a mean smile on the man's ferret-face. At that moment what must have been the barrel of Hendrik's rifle crashed down on Longarm's head.

Oh, shit, he thought as he crashed through the floor into oblivion.

Chapter 9

When Longarm's senses returned, his head was pounding. He wasn't sure if it was from the blow on his head or the moonshine. He sat up very carefully and gingerly probed the back of his head until his fingers found the lump where the rifle barrel had come down. It was exquisitely sensitive, and he realized he would appreciate a cup of Hendrik's moonshine to help restore his enthusiasm for getting back up on his feet. The smell of moldy hay and horse manure was all around him, but there was no light at all. He might as well have been flung into a mine shaft.

Then he heard it again, the sound that had awakened him—a woman's tiny, enfeebled cry. Close by. He reached out blindly. His fingers struck a grain sack. Its rotted fibers broke and grain spilled out onto his hand. He was in the barn's storeroom, then. The soft cry came again, barely audible above the drunken laughter that came from the cabin. He stood up and groped toward the sound until he came to the storeroom's wall, then kept moving along it until he reached a door.

Leaning his head against it, he called out softly, "Who's there?"

"Mr. Long!" a girl whispered hoarsely. "It's me. Irene!"

"Irene? What in blazes are you doing out here?"

"Please. Help me," she pleaded.

"First things first. Get me out of this room."

"It's padlocked from this side."

"Go find a crowbar—anything to pry off the latch."

He heard her move off and waited, his body leaning against the door. He was still shaky, and his head continued to pound with undiminished enthusiasm. After what seemed like a generation, Irene returned.

"Mr. Long!"

"Did you get a crowbar?"

"Yes. But . . . I can hardly lift it."

"See if you can push it under the door."

She tried at three or four places, then succeeded finally in pushing a portion of the crowbar's snout under it. On his knees Longarm caught hold of the crowbar and pulled it all the way into the grainery. It was heavy, all right, he realized as he got to his feet and steadied himself in front of the door.

"Stand back," he told Irene.

Careful to make as little noise as possible, he pried at the door's edge in an effort to spring the nails buried in the door frame. As he heaved on the crowbar, his head spun wildly, and twice he let the crowbar thud to the room's dirt floor. On his third heave, however, the nails holding the latch squealed and popped free. The lock and hasp dropped to the floor and the door sagged open.

Longarm stood silently in the open doorway for a full moment, listening for any sign that his exertions might have been overheard by Hendrik or Dimmy. But there was no diminution of their wild, booming laughter, which was punctuated every now and then by the crash of something hitting the floor—followed invariably by peals of howling laughter.

Irene hurried to his side. She was close to panic. "Please, Mr. Long! You must get me away from them. They'll be coming for me again!"

"Irene, you don't have to call me mister. Remember? We're not exactly strangers."

"Just help me get away from here!"

"I heard you. But what in tarnation are you doing here, Irene?"

"I'm here because of you."

"Me?"

"It was Dimmy. He did it. He broke into my apartment. He was asleep on my couch when I came upstairs. I tried to get rid of him, but he took me in my own bed. Then he kidnapped me. He thought you'd come for me if you knew I was here. Then he'd kill you and get in real good with Slattery. For most of the day they've been passing me back and forth between them." She choked back sobs. "They are so *unclean!* So *filthy!*"

"Quiet, Irene. You'll bring them out here."

"It don't matter. They've heard my tears. All day they've heard them."

"And so I rode up here anyway. Right into Dimmy's hands."

"I was in the barn. I watched you ride up. I thought you came for me."

"Make believe I did, Irene. I would have, believe me, if Dimmy had contacted me. I would not have left you here, not with that animal."

She brightened pathetically. "Even though I'm so . . . fat?"

He put his arms around her and drew her close, then held her for a few minutes. Smoothing her hair, he said softly, "You're not fat. Not at all. You're just right." He kissed her tenderly on the lips.

She rested her forehead on his chest. "Thank you, Custis," she said, her voice catching. "You're very kind."

It didn't matter if what he had told her was true or not, just so it was said. It was what she needed to hear. But even as he spoke, he realized he wasn't lying to her; he meant every word.

"Irene, why did they leave you loose out here? And why didn't Dimmy kill me when he had the chance?"

"They didn't leave me loose. Dimmy tied me up in the loft and stuffed a dishcloth in my mouth to keep me quiet. But he was so drunk he did a poor job, so I got loose about an hour ago. And Dimmy didn't kill you when you rode up because he was up in the loft with me. Besides, he doesn't want to kill you until tomorrow."

"Why tomorrow?"

"While he tied me back up, he told me they're going to ride back to the Lazy C with you. When they get a few miles from it, Dimmy's going to club you senseless and hang you from a stirrup, then whip your horse to a gallop."

"And by the time it gets back to the Lazy C, my boot will be all that's left."

108

"Yes," she said, shuddering.

"Nice. That should put Dimmy in real good with his boss. And the best part is it would look like an accident." He looked around the darkened barn. "Where's my horse?"

"In the stall on the other side."

"Lead the way."

When they reached the stall, Longarm saw that his mount had not even been unsaddled, just led into the stall and forgotten. Its head was drooping and the reins were tangled at its feet. He eased into the stall past the animal and gently took the bit from its mouth, then backed the horse out. His bedroll was still tied to the saddle. To give the horse some relief, he took off the saddle and the bedroll, peeled off the saddle blanket and spent a few minutes rubbing the horse down. Then he found a bucket and sneaked out to the pump. The wild laughter from the house was easily loud enough to cover the squeak of the pump handle. After he watered the horse, he grained it. Then he put the saddle blanket back on and saddled the horse, led it out of the rear of the barn and tethered it to a corral post.

"But I can't ride," said Irene.

"Then you'll just have to ride up on the cantle behind me and hang on."

"Don't worry. I will."

A harsh bark of laughter filled the night. It sounded much louder than before, and Longarm realized the two men had spilled out of the cabin and were heading for the barn. And why not? That's where they had left their prisoner—and their blond plaything.

"Stay here," Longarm told Irene.

He slipped back into the barn and searched for and found a kerosene lantern. Lighting it, he tossed it high into the hayloft. It took only seconds for the hay to catch. With a soft, but ominous *whump,* flames swept through the loft.

With the fire flaring above him, Longarm darted back out the rear of the barn, then circled it. He was just in time to see Hendrik and Dimmy throwing up their arms to protect themselves as they rushed into the barn to save their horses. Longarm entered the cabin and picked up his .44-40 off the kitchen table. He dropped it into his holster, grabbed one of Hendrik's kerosene lanterns, and flung it against a wall, then picked another one off the table and let that fly as well. Sheets of flame leapt up the walls and began licking at the ceiling.

But not even the fires of hell could burn off that awful stench, he thought as he ran from the cabin. As he neared the corner of the barn, Hendrik and Dimmy emerged from it, leading their horses. They were carrying their saddles and were bent close to the horses' flanks to shield themselves from the black coils of smoke pouring out through the open barn door. Once out of the barn, they led their horses toward the cottonwoods.

Longarm kept on to the back of the barn, where Irene was huddled anxiously beside the now skittish horse. The flames had broken through the barn's roof by this time and were so bright it seemed that daylight had come early; the grass was a bright green, and Irene's blond hair gleamed.

He mounted up and reached down to grab Irene's wrist.

"Put your left foot into that stirrup," he told her. "I'll haul you up behind me. Then wrap your arms around my waist."

As he held her hand, she lifted her left foot and tucked it into the stirrup.

"Ready?" he asked her.

"Yes," she whispered.

But he never got the chance to haul her up behind him. Someone's head slammed into his back. As Irene screamed, he was dragged brutally off the horse, Nils Hendrik clinging to his back. They landed so heavily that Hendrik lost his grip on Longarm and rolled off him. Longarm jumped to his feet a second before Dimmy cracked full force into him, driving him violently back. Longarm stumbled, went down, rolled away from the flailing Dimmy, and jumped to his feet just in time to take Hendrik's second charge, which slammed him back against the barn. As flaming cinders rained down on him, he slipped under Hendrik's wild, drunken punches and drove his boot into Hendrik's groin. He buckled. Longarm brought his knee up, this time catching Hendrik in the face, and he felt the man's nose explode into mush. Stepping back, he kicked Hendrik in the chops. This took all the fight out of Hendrik and he sagged to the ground, blood bubbling from his broken face. Longarm took him by his suspenders and dragged him a safe distance from the barn.

As he was straightening up, he heard Irene scream out a warning. He turned to see her lunging desperately at him. Beyond her—less than ten feet away—Dimmy was sighting down his Colt's barrel at Longarm. At that distance he could not miss. Irene struck Longarm then, intent on pushing him out of

111

the line of fire. Dimmy's revolver detonated. Irene cried out and sagged against Longarm as she caught the bullet in her back. Longarm drew his .44 and fired back at Dimmy. But his shot went wild and before he could fire again, Dimmy had vanished behind a corner of the barn. Longarm heard him running for the cottonwoods.

He carried Irene away from the barn and let her down gently onto the ground. As the flames from the two burning buildings roared up into the night sky, they afforded Longarm enough light for him to see clearly the extent of Irene's wound. Dimmy's round had entered her back just under her right shoulder blade, ranged down through her lung, and emerged beneath her left breast, creating as jagged and ugly an exit wound as he had ever seen.

If Irene was lucky, she would die quickly.

Longarm heard Dimmy galloping off into the night just as Hendrik began to groan. He left Irene, walked over to Hendrik, and kicked him in the side, hard.

Hendrik's eyes flickered open. Longarm bent over him.

"Can you hear me, Hendrik?"

Hendrik nodded.

"Then listen to me. And listen good. Your barn is gone and so is your house. You're burned out. You got no choice now but to clear out of this valley. After tonight, if I ever see you again I will probably kill you."

Hendrik glanced past Longarm at Irene. "Dimmy do that?"

"Yes."

"I'll go," he mumbled, sitting up, "soon's I get my possibles. I don't even have a gun."

"Forget your possibles. Or any weapons," Longarm told him with brutal directness. "They're going up in flames right now."

Hendrik lurched to his feet. His face was ruined. His nose had been flattened, one eye was closed— and blood from his swollen lips had already begun to cake on his chin. He staggered off toward the cottonwoods.

Longarm went back to Irene, carried her still further from the searing heat, and placed her gently down on the cool grass. For a long while he watched her face. From the deep hollows in her cheeks and the chalk white of her complexion, he knew she was going fast.

He heard the soft thunder of Hendrik's horse. It faded quickly.

Irene opened her eyes.

"You are not hurt, Custis?" she asked, her voice a tiny whisper.

"I'm fine."

She smiled, pleased. "Then he didn't shoot you."

"Dammit, Irene, he shot you instead. That was a very brave, very foolish thing you did."

"You aren't angry with me?"

"Of course not."

"Kiss me," she said softly, "the way you did in the barn. It was so gentle, so sweet."

He bent close and kissed her again, as gently as before. When her lips released his a moment later they were already growing cold.

Early the next morning Longarm found a spot on a knoll overlooking the broadest reaches of the valley. A smoky purple in the distance, the snowcapped peaks

113

that flanked the valley were suspended miraculously in the sky like majestic sentinels. The scent of sage and wild peppers filled the air. A moment before he had seen a doe step cautiously from a patch of timber. The song of a hermit thrush echoed over the slope.

With the charred remains of a shovel he had taken from Hendrik's ruined barn, he dug a grave and lowered Irene's slicker-wrapped body into it. To prevent wolves or coyotes from digging her body up, he piled stones upon the grave, constructing a burial cairn all who passed by would recognize as such.

Then he doffed his hat and said a silent prayer for the woman who had given her life for his.

Chapter 10

Horsehead's single main street was quietly watchful as Longarm rode. It was close to sundown. Clots of gun-heavy hard cases on both sides of the street gathered to watch him ride past. Some Longarm recognized as former Lazy C riders, but others he did not recognize. Slattery was bringing in more gunslicks, it appeared. Longarm kept on until he reached the saloon, then turned his horse into the hitch rail and swung down.

He had just finished mounting the saloon's steps when Slattery, Dimmy, and the the sheriff pushed through the batwings and paused, blocking his way. Standing between the burly sheriff and Slattery, Dimmy had a nervous smile on his face, reminding Longarm of a cat licking its chops after swallowing a mouse. The palm of his right hand rested lightly on the butt of his six-gun.

"You killed her, Dimmy," Longarm said to him. "Irene took the bullet you meant for me."

"I didn't tell her to jump in front of you."

"You must be crazy, Long," said Slattery. "Ridin' in here like this as naked as a plucked chicken, no one siding you."

Longarm could feel as well as hear the gathering ring of gunslicks edging up behind him in the street.

"I'm only interested in Dimwit, here," Longarm told Slattery.

Slattery chuckled. "Dimwit, hey? That's good. I never thought of that. You got a real sense of humor, Long. But that don't change nothin'. You're still fresh meat to a hungry man, ridin' in here like this."

"You want to cut down on me, Slattery, go ahead. You got all the firepower you need. But think a moment. I won't go down quiet, and before I do there's a good chance a stray bullet will find you and Dimwit here."

The sheriff looked nervously at Slattery and edged a few inches to one side.

"Don't listen to him, boss," Dimmy said. "We can take him."

"What do you mean *we*, Dimwit?" Slattery snapped. "He's *your* problem. You're the one cut Irene down. You know how long it'll take to get someone to run that restaurant, now she's gone?" Slattery turned to Longarm, a conciliatory smile on his face. "Now, why don't we just hold it a minute here, Long. There ain't no need for gunplay. I'm a fair man. I got no grudge with you. So I'll hold my mad dogs in check here and let you ride out of this valley, away from all this unpleasantness."

"You sayin' you'll let me ride out?"

"You heard me."

"That's real decent of you." Longarm appeared to relax then. "But what about Dimwit here? You think he'll let you do that? Besides, maybe I should stay on in here. This valley might be just the place I'm lookin' for."

Slattery's eyes narrowed. "What do you mean by that?"

"I mean you must've ridden in here like I did, Slattery, looking for action, hoping to change your luck. I been a saddle tramp long enough. Maybe it's time I settled down."

Slattery chuckled meanly. "You mean you think this valley can hold both of us?"

"Not while Dimwit still draws a breath in it. You and I won't have no problems, Slattery, once we sit down and settle our differences. But Dimwit's got to go."

"You call me Dimwit one more time, Long, and I'll blast you right here."

"Will you?"

Before Dimmy could get his gun out of his holster, Slattery pinned his arms while the sheriff lifted Dimmy's six-gun from his holster.

"Holy Jesus, Slattery!" Dimmy cried, beside himself with frustration. "We got guns all around this bastard. We can take him!"

"I don't want no gunplay, Dimwit."

"You can't do this!"

"Looks to me like I'm already doing it."

Slattery let Dimmy go and shoved him halfway down the steps.

"Get on your horse, Dimmy," Slattery told him coldly. "Ride out and keep riding. And I don't want to have to repeat myself."

As Slattery spoke he rested his right hand on the butt of his own six-gun. His face a scalded red, Dimmy flung one last, murderous glance at Longarm, then backed his horse away from the hitch rack and swung aboard.

"I want my weapon," he told Slattery.

Slattery tossed it to him. Dimmy caught it, dropped it into his holster, then yanked his horse about and left town at full gallop.

Slattery looked shrewdly at Longarm.

"Am I right, Long? You want to deal?"

"Why do you think I rode in here?"

"Come inside. It's cooler and after all that upset, I'm thirsty."

Longarm followed Slattery into the saloon's cool interior. When Slattery turned and saw Sheriff Belcher trailing in after them, he held up and shook his head.

"We don't need you, Belcher."

"Sure, Slattery," the lawman said, backing hastily out of the saloon.

"That sure is one fierce lawman," Longarm said, as he slacked into a chair at a table along the wall.

"Ain't that the truth," Slattery said, sitting down beside him. "And Belcher still remembers you some. Good thing when you pitched him down those stairs he landed on his head. He might have hurt himself."

Emerald came over to see what they were drinking, then returned a moment later with their drinks. When she started to go back to the bar, Slattery asked her to join them. Her eyes warily fixed on Longarm, she sat down at the table.

She glanced at Slattery. "I just heard. Irene's dead."

"Yeah, Dimmy tried to kill Long here and shot her instead. A real loss to the community."

118

"My God, Buck, who's going to run the restaurant?"

"Maybe you could add that to your list of accomplishments."

"Not on your life. This place is enough and more than enough for me to handle."

"One of your girls, then."

"I suppose," Emerald said, frowning in thought. "Now that I think of it, Anna's getting a mite frazzled around the edges."

"And she's puttin' on lard. But can she run a restaurant?"

"She's already got a cook. What more does she need? Don't worry. She can handle it."

And that appeared to settle the problem of Irene's untimely death. Longarm was chilled inwardly as he saw how matter-of-fact the solution had been to Irene's loss.

Slattery turned to Longarm. "Dimmy told me about the deal you were peddling with Hendrik. Is Rosita serious? Is she really willing to give some of her cattle back?"

"That's her offer. Split up her ill-gotten gains with the other ranchers; then maybe they'll throw in with her. I told her it was a crazy idea, but she insisted. So I spent the day riding out to the Bench and the Bar N with her proposal."

"You have any luck?"

"Nope."

Slattery nodded. "I guess I worried too much about them two ranchers. Not a one has the backbone to buck me."

"Not after you let them know you'd close off the town to them."

"Spineless bastards. All of them."

"I gotta admit. That's the way I'm beginning to see it, too."

"Outside there, you said you're sick of being a saddle tramp, that you might be ready to make a deal. You mean that?"

"Maybe."

"Before we go any further, there's one thing I want to know."

"What's that?"

"I got a wound in my left side. Rosita did it. Was it you gave her that gun?"

"I gave it to her."

"Then it was you chased me off her before that."

"That was me, all right."

He leaned back in his chair and regarded Longarm coolly. "I knew it was. I just wanted to see if you'd level with me. Dimmy told me it was you."

"He was at the Lazy C when I rode in."

"How come you're willing to cross Rosita? That's a lot of woman there—and that's the best spread in the valley."

"I'm not so willing. Don't like to do it. She trusts me. But I saw yesterday how much help she can count on from the other ranchers—and besides, when I wanted some kind of a thank you for what I done, she pulled rank on me. It didn't set well."

Slattery grinned. "Yeah. She's real uppity. I found that out myself."

"That so, Buck?" Emerald said, glancing sidelong at him, the trace of a smile on her hard lips. "And here I thought you said that Mex wasn't wasn't worth the bother."

Slattery glanced at her. "I lied. There ain't a woman alive who ain't worth the bother—when a man gets urgent enough."

Emerald chuckled. "True enough, Slattery. True enough."

Slattery looked back at Longarm. "I saw what Hendrik looked like after you got done with him. He was in town early this morning. I never saw anyone in such a hurry to ride out of this valley. As soon as he could get provisioned, he left at a gallop. I never thought I'd see the man who could take that ape down a peg, but you did it."

"You like that, huh?"

"Thing is, you got balls, Long. And like you found out yesterday, that's in short supply around here. So what's your price for throwing in with me and my men?"

Longarm pulled his beer closer and sipped it thoughtfully. "That depends."

"On what?"

"On what you're offering."

"I'll make it as sweet as I can. You keep out of the way while I make my move on the Lazy C and you'll be a saddle tramp no more. I'll let you stay in the valley."

"Hell, Slattery. I've already decided to stay."

"All right then. I'll give you the Bar H spread."

"Shit, that's hardscrabble country up there. Short grass and little water." Longarm grinned thinly. "And someone just burnt the place down—the house and the barn."

"Okay, so you'll have to put up new buildings. But that won't be no problem. Besides, you don't think you could've lived in Hendrik's cabin, do you? When the wind was right we could smell it all the way down here."

Longarm shook his head. "That's not good enough, Slattery."

Slattery leaned back in his chair and regarded Longarm shrewdly. He knew Longarm was close to making a deal. The only question was, what would it take to push him over the edge.

"Aw, hell," Slattery drawled. "I want you the hell out of my hair. You've been trouble from the beginning. Forget Hendrik's place. What'd you think of the Bar N?"

"Dan Wilson's place."

"Yeah."

"Good land and lots of it. Well watered. Not a bad spread."

"And I'll throw in a couple of hundred head of Lazy C."

"How you going to be able to do all that?"

"Simple. After I get back into the Lazy C, Dan Wilson will be next. You already know what he's made of. One huff and I'll blow his house down." He grinned at the thought.

"All right," he said. "It's a deal."

The two men shook hands.

Emerald spoke up then. "Besides keeping out of Slattery's way, Long, what else are you going to do for all this landscape and livestock?"

"And for me letting you live," Slattery added with a grin.

"Help."

"I'm listening."

"De Santos is no fool. He wasn't hurt bad when you tried to take him out and he's already up and

122

about. He's got his men looking sharp, and they'll bust their asses to protect Rosita. You won't find it easy to ride in there and ruin their stores and run off their livestock. You might even have to burn down that mansion—and if I'm not mistaken, that's what you want the most."

Slattery took Emerald's hand. "Em here would like that place. She already told me that."

"So what kind of help are you offering, Long?" Emerald persisted.

"A plan that would give you what you want with one quick stroke."

"Go on," said Slattery.

"I'll ride back to the Lazy C. When we're ready I'll create a diversion. A fire. One of their barns, maybe, or the bunkhouse. De Santos's men will be so busy trying to put out the flames, they won't have time to put up any resistance when you and your men ride in."

Slattery's eyes met Emerald's. Longarm saw agreement flash between them.

Slattery looked back at Longarm. "It's so damn simple, it'll have to work. I like it."

"There's one thing more."

"What's that?"

"I want this in writing. The entire deal. Including your promise to deed me the Bar N—plus the cattle. We can call it a contract."

Slattery frowned and leaned back in his chair. "You mean my word's not good enough for you?"

"Not after what I've been through. That's why I'm on the run. I trusted too many fast-talking con men."

"You ain't calling me a con man, are you?"

"Not if you're willing to put our deal on paper and sign it."

"Is that all it would take?" Emerald asked.

"That's all."

"Hell," Emerald told Slattery. "That ain't no problem, Buck. I can write it out. Let's go into the office."

With a shrug, Slattery got to his feet and followed Emerald as she led the way to the office. As Slattery closed the door behind them, Emerald went around behind her desk, sat down, and pulled some foolscap from a drawer. She selected a sheet, reached for a pen and a bottle of ink and began to write.

Slattery watched her uneasily, glancing occasionally at Long. Long could tell he didn't like this development and was going along with it only because Emerald seemed to think it was all right.

Finished, Emerald glanced up, blotted the paper on the desk blotter, then handed it to Slattery. He read it slowly, his lips moving slightly. When he finished, he handed the contract back to Emerald. She in turn gave it to Longarm.

As he read it, he realized at once that Slattery was the brawn and Emerald the brains. The language sounded impressively legal. For services rendered, Longarm was to be given Dan Wilson's Bar N outfit as soon as Slattery regained effective control of the Lazy C, and the Bar N became available, at which time Slattery was to give Longarm five hundred head of Lazy C cattle in addition to whatever stock came with the Bar N holdings. The contract was binding on both parties for the next six months. At the bottom of the page was a line drawn for Slattery's signature, and beneath it, one for their new partner, Custis Long. At the bottom of the contract was a line for the witness's signature as well. The witness, obviously, would be Emerald.

Longarm glanced at Emerald. "I see there's no mention here of how we plan to restore Slattery's control over the Lazy C and take over the Bar N."

Emerald smiled. "I thought we'd leave that to the imagination."

Longarm reached for the pen, dipped it into the inkwell on her desk, and signed. Then he handed the pen and contract to Slattery, who scrawled his name above Longarm's. Emerald took it from him and carefully signed her name as the witness.

After folding it carefully, she placed it in the desk's bottom drawer. She closed the drawer on the contract and locked it, dropping the key into the top drawer under the blotter.

"Now how soon can you manage that diversion?" Slattery asked Longarm.

"Give me three days. Move in at midnight."

"All right. We'll go in as soon as we see the barn go up."

"It'll take some doing for me to get loose without alerting De Santos and his men, so don't panic if I don't get that fire going right at midnight."

"We'll give you an hour."

"That should be enough."

Slattery looked at Emerald and grinned. "How's that, Em? Looks like we'll be moving into that big ranch house soon."

"That'll suit me just fine," Emerald said. "This town is overrun with your gunslicks. They're wearing out my girls and drinking up all my whiskey. I need a rest and so does this town."

Longarm touched the brim of his hat to Emerald, bid good-bye to Slattery, then left the office and strode from the saloon. Outside, Slattery's grim clot of hard cases were still clustered in front of the saloon's entrance. They moved back grudgingly and watched him mount up without uttering a word. As he pulled his horse around and lifted it to a lope, he could feel their hard eyes on his back.

When at last the town vanished behind him, Longarm shuddered and took a deep breath. He felt as if he had just climbed out of a nest of rattlesnakes.

Back in Horsehead later that night, Longarm heard someone in the alley behind him. He whirled to see a shadowy figure looming out of the dark. He could not tell if the man had seen him. He ducked behind an outhouse and waited for the man to go on past him.

"Hey!" the man called, pulling up in front of the privy. "That you, Frank?" His words were slurred from too much firewater.

There was a muffled response from within the privy.

"Where the hell you been all this time? Them girls won't wait much longer!"

The outhouse door creaked open and Longarm heard a man stumble out. "For Christ's sake, Andy! Can't I take a crap without you naggin' me?"

Both men, obviously drunk, stumbled off down the alley.

Longarm waited until they were gone before he stepped out from behind the privy and continued on down the back alley. When he reached the Horsehead saloon, he found it dark, which was what he had expected this late. He found the window in Emerald's office, lifted the sash, boosted himself over the sill, and crouched down beside the window to listen. There might be someone still in the saloon. Emerald and Slattery, perhaps, drinking to their new partnership with Custis Long.

Longarm heard nothing. He moved on cat feet over to the door, listened with his ear against it for a moment longer, then turned back to the desk. His eyes by now had adjusted to the room's darkness. He pulled out the top drawer and felt around in it for the key. It was not there. He lit a match and held it over the desk.

The key was right in front of him on the green desk blotter. He snatched it up and opened the bottom drawer. Reaching in, he found the contract. The expensive foolscap on which it had been written was still impressively stiff and new. He lit another match, held it up to the paper, and read it over once more to make sure. Pleased, he placed it in the breast pocket of his jacket, then closed and locked the drawer. He dropped the key back onto the desk as close to possible on the spot where he had found it, then eased himself out through the window, closed it, and moved swiftly back up the alley.

His horse was tethered behind the feed mill. When he reached it, he mounted up quickly and rode unchallenged out of town, heading north for the Bar N. His hope now was that Emerald would not feel the need to check over the contract before Slattery made his move on the Lazy C.

Chapter 11

Dan Wilson was no happier to see Longarm a second time than he had been the first. Once again cradling a rifle, he stood with his wife on the porch as Longarm rode across the Bar N compound. Behind Longarm rode three Bar N riders, who had closed in behind him a mile back and without a word had escorted him to the ranch. The rest of Wilson's riders were waiting in the compound as well. No question about it, Slattery's earlier warning to Wilson had made him a very nervous man.

"Expecting trouble?" Longarm asked him, as he reined in before the hitch rack.

"What do you want, Long?"

"I want to talk to you."

"We already done that. We ain't nothin' more to talk about."

"Maybe we have, but you don't know it yet." Longarm glanced at his wife and touched his hat brim to her. "Howdy, ma'am. You got any coffee on?"

"I always do," Samantha said. "Light and set a spell."

Not quite sure if he should be pleased with his wife's offer of hospitality, Wilson followed her and Longarm into the house. Once the coffee was poured and the three of them were sitting around the kitchen table, Longarm took out the contract he and Slattery had signed and passed it to Dan Wilson without comment. Wilson unfolded the foolscap, read the contract with growing anger, then passed it to Samantha. When she finished, her face was tight with outrage. She thrust it back at Longarm, who took it and placed it down beside his cup.

"You are a strange man, Mr. Long," Samantha said, "to come here so brazenly with such a document in hand."

Wilson said, "I'd like an explanation, Long,"

"I got that contract from Buck Slattery by promising to help him take over the Lazy C. As this contract makes clear, he's promised to give me your ranch in payment for my services."

"But that makes no sense!" Wilson said angrily. "The Bar N is not his to give. Not to anyone!"

"Not now, it isn't."

"Then what . . ."

"Can't you see it, Wilson? Buck Slattery plans to take over this entire valley. The town is filling up with gunslicks. With my help, he expects to take over the biggest spread in the valley. And there's no one to stop him. What little law there is up here is on his side, no matter what he does. So if he wants to pay me off with your ranch, what's to stop him?"

"Why are you telling us this," Samantha asked, "if you're on his side?"

130

"Because I'm not on his side. Not really. With this contract I'm showing you what you're up against. You and the Lazy C. That's why we need your help."

"But if we help the Lazy C," Wilson said, "Slattery will only come down on us all that quicker."

"Sooner or later, he'll ruin you, Wilson. Unless you stop him now. Seems to me you have only one way out of this."

"Yes," Samantha said, pouring Longarm another cup of coffee. "We must help the Lazy C and fight him. Now."

"All right," said Wilson. "I guess Samantha is right."

"You're in?"

"Just tell me what you've go up your sleeve."

"For now I want you to ride over to Jack French and convince him to throw in with us. We'll need him and his men. If he argues, show him this contract and explain it to him the way I just did to you. Remember that if Slattery is thinking of running you off the Bar N, he has the same plans for the Bench."

"Do it, Dan," said Samantha. "Jack will listen to you."

"Then," Longarm continued, "as soon as you can—by tomorrow at the latest—bring your men and French's outfit with you to the Lazy C."

"What then, Long?"

"When Slattery makes his move on the Lazy C, we'll have a noisy surprise for him and his gunslicks."

Wilson nodded grimly. It appeared that once he had made his decision to throw in with Long, there were no more doubts. In fact, Wilson seemed almost

eager now to take part in the dismantling of Buck
Slattery.

"I'll ride to the Bench immediately," he told
Longarm.

Longarm handed the contract to Wilson, finished
his coffee, and got to his feet.

"Thanks for the coffee, Samantha."

She smiled, and in that instant her plain, care-
worn face looked surprisingly radiant.

"Custis Long," she said. "I think we're going to be
friends."

"Partners, at least," agreed Wilson, getting to his
feet also.

Longarm left the house and mounted up. He waved
to the Wilson's and rode out, heading back to the
Lazy C. He had ridden through the night and was
close to exhaustion. His only hope now was that he
could remain in the saddle until he arrived back at
the Lazy C.

Longarm sat up in the huge bed, frowning.

"What's that?" he asked.

"It's a bathtub, Custis," Rosita told him.

"It sure is a fancy item."

"It's a lady's bathtub," she told him. "But it should
do nicely for you."

"It's too small."

"You'll just have to pull in your legs some."

Rosita and Blossom had just set the bathtub down
beside the bed. It bore no resemblance to the big
corrugated steel tubs Longarm frequented in the
back rooms of barber shops. This tub had a graceful, flaring backrest from the back of which hung a
towel rack, and on its enameled surface had been

painted rosebuds with small robins flitting among the branches.

Blossom hurried out for the water.

"Hadn't you better get undressed?" Rosita asked him impishly.

Longarm threw back the covers, unbuttoned his undershirt, and peeled out of his long johns.

"Oh my," Rosita said softly, staring at his crotch. "Was all that inside me?"

He stood boldly before her. "All of it."

Blossom returned with two steaming buckets. Without a glance at Longarm, she emptied them into the bathtub, then left the room for more. When she had poured in about five more buckets, it was ready for Longarm. He stepped carefully into it and sank slowly into the steaming water. Beads of perspiration popped out on his forehead. He could almost feel the encrusted dirt lifting off his skin.

"Close the door behind you, Blossom," Rosita said.

Blossom left, pulling the door securely shut, and Rosita knelt on a cushion beside the tub, a long-handled back brush in one hand and a bar of soap in the other.

"I can wash myself," Longarm said, reaching for the soap.

"I know you can," Rosita said. "But you did me a favor once, so now I'm going to do you one."

She began to soap his head. Stinging suds flowed down his forehead into his eyes. He blinked painfully, but kept his composure. Without warning, she shoved his head forward into the water. Blowing like a whale, he pushed his head up out of it. She laughed, then pushed his head down again, keeping it there for what seemed an eternity while she rinsed the soap off his head. He was gasping when she finally allowed him up.

"You trying to drown me?"

"Now don't be such a sissy. Don't you want your hair washed?"

"It's the drowning I don't like."

"Hush now and close your eyes." .

He shut them just in time as she picked up a steaming bucket of water Blossom had left and poured it over his head and shoulders. The shock of it caused Longarm to lose his breath momentarily. Gasping, he shook himself off like a wet dog and started to scramble from the tub. Laughing, Rosita pushed him back down, reached into the steaming water for the brush and soap and began scrubbing his back.

Longarm sighed happily. This was more like it. He glanced at Rosita and saw that she was making no effort to conceal her admiration of his broad shoulders and the hard, ribbed muscles of his back. She pushed him back against the backrest and began scrubbing his shoulders and chest—and further down.

All the way down.

"Oh, my . . ." she murmured. "It's so big."

Her strong fingers closed mischievously about his erection, her flushed face close to Longarm's. Without conscious volition he fastened his lips to hers. They parted and she leaned into him, her hand working expertly now. He put his wet arms about her and pulled her closer. The rapid movement of her hand caused the water to splash some, but neither paid any attention. Then he gasped and cried out, still clinging to her. Delighted, she pulled away and let him lean back against the tub's backrest. Drained, he regarded her through lidded eyes.

"Can you stand up now?" she asked.

"Give me a minute."

She laughed. He got to his feet.

"I seem to have diminished you," she commented as she soaped his thighs, the backs of his legs, his ankles, and his feet. "What strange power do we women possess over such big strong men?"

"Just don't let it go to your head," he warned her, grinning.

After rinsing him off with a bucket of steaming water, she dried him off with a body towel. As soon as he stepped out of the tub, he took her in his arms and carried her over to the bed. He was still not entirely dry, but she did not protest as he unbuttoned her dress and helped her remove her shift and frilly drawers. At last she was naked under him.

And he was no longer diminished.

Longarm used the large dining room table to illustrate his plan. Wilson stood at his right, Jack French and De Santos on the other side of the table, Rosita beside him on his left. He had already set up knives and forks for boundaries. A sugar bowl represented Horsehead. Salt and pepper shakers stood for the Lazy C. A cream pitcher represented the rustled herd Slattery and his men had hidden in the high valleys.

Longarm had just asked Wilson about them. Wilson had sent two of his riders out to check on it earlier in the day.

"The cattle are still up there, with only a couple of Slattery's men guarding them."

"Good," said Longarm.

Jack French frowned. "What's that herd got to do with this business?"

"I plan to use it to flush out the town."

"Flush out Horsehead?"

"He means a stampede," said Rosita, smiling.

"I'll explain later," Longarm told French.

French shrugged and looked back down at the table as Longarm continued to outline his plan.

"As soon as we light that pile of old lumber and fence posts behind the barn," he told them, "Slattery will be on his way. The important thing is not to open up on Slattery's force until they're inside the Lazy C compound. We'll be the ones to open fire—but not until he's securely in the trap. Pick off as many as we can, then take after them when they retreat to Horsehead."

"If they do," said Wilson nervously.

"Sure, they will. We'll make mincemeat of them," said Jack French.

Longarm looked across the table at De Santos. Though Longarm had not wanted the old Mexican to join them, since he was not yet fully recovered from his wound, De Santos had insisted on being included.

"Eduardo," Longarm said, "you and your men will be waiting in the gap when Slattery heads back through it on his way back to Horsehead. Open up on him then with all you've got."

Eduardo nodded, pleased at this important deployment. "Si, we will cut Slattery and his men to pieces."

"As for me," Longarm said, "I will be in the hills with those Bar N riders Wilson has lent me. When

Slattery makes his move on the Lazy C, I'll be driving that herd into Horsehead."

"But after all this," Jack French said, "will that be necessary?"

"Look at it this way. We're not likely to bring down every one of Slattery's riders tonight, and in all the confusion, there's a good chance we'll miss Slattery as well. He's gotten out of tighter scrapes than this, I'm thinking. But what we *can* do is destroy his base, give him no place from which to mount another attack on the Lazy C, or any other outfit in this valley. Wipe out his nest completely. The saloon, the mill, the general store—everything."

"Wait a minute," said Wilson. "If we do that, how will we provision ourselves afterward?"

"The provisions will still be there, and so will the mill, though not in a very tidy condition, I admit. But after the dust settles, there's a good chance the present or future owners will take heed of their customers, not Buck Slattery."

"Seems pretty damn complicated," Dan Wilson said, frowning.

"I don't think so," said Longarm quietly. "We lure Slattery into a trap here." He pointed to the salt and pepper shakers. "Then we drive him back through the gap, where Eduardo and his men cut him down some more. Then we take away his base of operations. With that gone, he's no longer a force to be reckoned with in this valley."

Rosita spoke up then. "And we will have shown how well we can defend ourselves together." Her eyes swept the table. "Never again will another Buck Slattery and his gunmen ride into this valley and take over.

Dan Wilson caught her eyes. "And your offer still goes?"

"You mean for me to break up my herds and distribute them equally among you? Of course. It is the only fair thing to do."

Jack French beamed at her.

Looking around the table, Longarm realized that the time for talk had passed. It was close to midnight. They were ready to set the bonfire.

"Any trouble?" Longarm asked, as he rode up to Ben.

"One of Slattery's men pulled out his Colt, but when he saw how many of us there were, he dropped it. The other one with him offered no resistance at all. He was just pleased to stay alive."

"Where are they now?"

"Hog-tied over there," Ben said, pointing to a small stand of timber halfway up the slope. "In among those trees. They should be able to wiggle loose some time tomorrow, we figure."

Longarm had put Ben in charge of the Bar N riders. They hadn't liked it much, but they had no choice in the matter. Ben had been outfitted with a new revolver and gunbelt, and he had stuck his small crowbar in his belt—just in case, he told Longarm.

"Well, let's go then," Longarm told him.

They angled down the slope and cautiously approached the herd. The waiting Bar N riders had circled it, and about the herd's fringe Longarm could see the glow of cigarettes where the riders sat their horses.

He waved them over to him.

"We're moving out now," he told them as soon as they reached him. "But remember, we don't want a stampede until we get to the outskirts of town—and then I want these brutes to go right down the main street, and back again if need be."

The riders nodded and pulled their mounts around. A moment later a chorus of ragged whistles filled the night. A few unhappy cattle began to low, and then the heaving backs began to move down the slope in a dark, massive wedge—on their way to flush out Horsehead.

Longarm glanced up at the stars. It was pretty damn close to midnight.

Slattery chuckled as he and his men raced toward the glowing sky. From the light of the burning building he could already make out the ranch house itself and a few of the other buildings. The layout of the Lazy C was as familiar to him as the palm of his hand. He knew where every building was, including the storehouse, the bunkhouse, blacksmith shop— even those chicken coops in back.

When he pounded through the gate into the compound, he expected to see the Lazy C hands rushing about with water buckets as they tried to save the burning barn. But it was not the barn that was on fire. The flames were coming from *behind* it! One of his men pulled alongside him and shouted that it was a trap. But he had already figured that out.

Long had double-crossed him!

"Pull up!" he cried to his men. "Go back! Ride out of here!"

But it was too late. At his cry, the night around him came alive with gunfire. Slattery felt as well as heard a slug whip past his cheek. He wheeled his horse and headed for the gate, firing at the muzzle flashes as he rode. But the hail of lead became even more devastating as he neared the gate. He saw two of his men peel of their mounts and realized the futility of trying to ride back the way they had come. He turned his horse aside, heading for the cover of the horse barn. His men were milling about in the middle of the compound, demoralized by the withering fire pouring at them from all sides. As Slattery rode through their ranks, he did his best to rally them.

"Go for the barn!" he urged. "We ain't finished yet!"

Grateful for Slattery's direction, his riders followed him in a charge at the barn, those that could. Before they pounded through the barn's open door, two more riders had tumbled from their mounts.

Crouched down behind the pump house, Rosita was so excited—and terrified—she could hardly breathe. The night was filled with desperation and death. The wild pounding of horses' hooves and the steady rattle of gunfire filled the night. Her soul quaked at the whine of hot lead and the shouts of desperate and dying men that came from every side.

She had insisted on being the one to set the lumber pile afire. Now that she saw what that action had wrought, she could only tremble in horrified fascination. She had watched Slattery try to ride back out through the gate, had watched him retreat, rally his men and ride into the barn in the face of the Lazy C riders who had been deployed there. Now Slattery and most of his men were trapped inside the barn.

They would never get out of this compound alive.

She had been carrying a rifle from the first, but had not yet fired a single shot. This made her feel guilty for not carrying her weight. Compressing her lips in grim determination, she moved cautiously out from behind the water trough in order to add her firepower to the Lazy C men who were pouring a steady fire into the barn.

One of Slattery's men burst from the barn and headed directly for the water trough. He ran hard, his head down. It was clear he had no idea she was using it for cover. Dodging gunfire as he ran, he grew closer and closer. At first she thought he would be cut down before he reached the trough. But he kept on, miraculously untouched by the intense fire directed at him.

At last she realized it was up to her to stop him. She stood up and raised the rifle, trying desperately to catch his weaving figure in her sights. Without warning, someone struck her from the side and dragged her to the ground. She struggled to get free and saw that it was Jack French who was holding her down.

"Keep down!" he told her.

He released her then and raised his six-gun and fired at another of Slattery's men who had been coming at her from the side. Struck in the stomach, the man coughed and plunged on past her, staggering crookedly as he vanished into the night. Then French spun to face the other one still making his dash for the horse trough. French fired at him point-blank. The running man's hat flew off, but his head still down, he kept on coming. Two more shots from French's revolver finally slowed him. His legs turned to rope. He staggered and fell facedown, coming to rest less than a foot from the water trough.

"This here's a bad spot," Jack French told Rosita, pulling her to her feet. "It's too exposed. Make for the smithy's shop!"

As they ducked inside it a moment later, they heard a cry and saw Slattery, at the head of a much-reduced force, burst from the rear of the barn. The corral gates had already been opened by his men and through it Slattery and his riders swept, heading out into the lower pastures.

Rosita sighed with relief. Slattery and his men had broken out. They were gone. The nightmare was over.

Or was it?

From all around her came the cries of wounded men and the terrible, frantic whinnying of downed horses.

Chapter 12

Emerald swore softly. Then she straightened up and swore again, this time louder. The bottom drawer was empty. The contract was gone.

Swiftly she looked about the office as if expecting to find Long hovering in one of the room's corners. She went to the window and raised it. It had been shut, but not snugly, not the way she usually left it. The dirty bastard had got in this way. How long ago, she wondered—then realized it didn't matter.

Slamming down the window, Emerald shook her head bitterly. They had intended to tear up the contract as soon as Buck left for the Lazy C and leave Long out in the cold for all his trouble. Only it looked like the son of a bitch was way ahead of them. All right. So he had the contract. Much good it would do him. There wasn't a court in the land would uphold it.

She walked back to the desk, bent, and closed the bottom drawer. Then, out of habit, she locked it. She was about to drop the key onto the desk when she heard the first faint rumbling. The floor boards began trembling ever so slightly. Dropping the key, she reached out and took hold of a corner of the desk. It too was trembling. A picture on the far wall shifted crookedly, then crashed to the floor. By now the rumbling sound—like that of an approaching freight train—grew even louder.

Could it be an earthquake?

She was frightened all of a sudden. She had never been in one, but she had heard terrifying stories. The rumbling reached a crescendo until—above the thundering, heart-constricting sound—there came the frantic bawling of cattle.

She ran from the office and out through the saloon. Whiskey bottles began toppling from their shelves behind the bar. She paid no attention as she flung herself out through the batwings. What she saw astounded and terrified her. The street was filled with a bellowing tide of maddened cattle. Even as she took this in, one wild-eyed steer, swept along by the bawling, stampeding brutes at its back, climbed up onto the saloon porch and charged blindly at her.

She ducked back into the saloon and took refuge behind the bar as the steer, its head low, charged through the batwings, taking most of the doorframe with it. Other steers followed the lead of this one and began pouring through an ever-widening hole in the front of the saloon. Once inside, the frantic, maddened beasts began milling wildly, reducing chairs and tables to splinters. Soon the stream of crazed steers became a torrent. The entire wall facing the street, sagged, then buckled. Added to the roar of the stampede was the sound of shattering glass and splintering wood. By then the steers were brushing against the bar, and she felt it begin to shift slightly.

Ned Riley and Chips—her barkeep and the house gambler—were halfway down the stairs, still in the act of dressing. Chips was pulling on his pants, Ned Riley his boots.

"What the hell's going on?" Riley called down to her.

"A stampede! Can't you see that?"

"In Horsehead, for Christ's sake?"

"What are them cows doin' in *here?*" Chips demanded, as if he were about to punish the perpetrator.

For a moment Emerald was as baffled as they were—until she remembered the stolen contract.

"Custis Long!" she cried. "He's the one did this! Tell the girls up there to stay put and get your guns and round up as many men as you can. That son of a bitch is using these cattle to take this town!"

"My God, Em," cried Ned. "We can't go down there. We'll get trampled!"

At that moment Emerald saw that one of the steers had found its way to the rear and was in the act of crashing through the wall. She reached down under the bar for the shotgun and a handful of cartridges. Breaking it open, she loaded swiftly, snapped the gun together and fired over the heads of the cattle. Frantic, eyes starting out of their heads, the steers began climbing over each other in a desperate effort to escape the saloon. She sent another shot over their heads and moved out from behind the bar.

She loaded and fired over their heads again. The cattle plunged away from her, saw the opening at the rear of the saloon and charged straight for it.

145

Before long, the cattle were running in a steady stream through the saloon out into the alley beyond. Reloading the shotgun, she waited for a break in the stream, then darted out onto what was left of the saloon porch and fired point-blank at the first steer headed her way.

It veered, plunged, and leaping over the backs of those nearest it, swept on past the saloon. Another steer being swept headlong toward the porch needed convincing as well. She aimed coolly and fired, aiming at the white patch on its forehead. The animal swung away, taking many of the maddened brutes with it. Reloading swiftly, she stood her ground, occasionally sending a blast of buckshot at the stampeding cattle to keep them going on past the saloon.

Ned Riley and Chips pulled up behind her on the porch. She glanced at them. Both men were strapping six-guns to their waists.

"Go find the sheriff," she shouted at them above the hellish thunder. "Get all the men you can! We've got to be ready when Long shows!"

"How we goin' to get through that?" Chips yelled back at her, staring at the steady flow of cattle rushing past the saloon.

"Use the back alley!"

They vanished back into the saloon.

Emerald turned back to the stampeding cattle. As she did, her heart skipped a beat. Farther down the street, the general store was ablaze, the garish flames leaping from its upper story windows adding still one more dimension of terror to this insane night. The flames drove the cattle to a further frenzy. Wide-eyed, heads lifted as they bawled in terror, they swept on past the blazing building; they were

146

so scared they were attempting to walk on the backs of those in front of them.

The porch shifted, then crumbled, as the heavy bodies sweeping past finally wore away its last support. Emerald's composure cracked as she felt the boards beneath her feet lift, then dip. The brawling, plunging torrent veered closer to her. She fired twice over their heads, but it did not seem to have any effect. She dug into her nightdress's pocket for more shells and found she had none. A steer was on the slanted porch headed blindly for her. With a tiny cry, she tossed the shotgun aside and tried to duck back into the saloon.

Instead, she felt herself being lifted as the steer gored her in the stomach and carried her into the saloon. There was no pain, only the sense that something hard and oddly curved had taken root under her ribs, and then she was tossed aside. She came down hard, face down in the floor's damp, tobacco-fouled sawdust, heard the pound of hooves behind her, felt the first hoof crunch into the small of her back, heard the crunch of bone as the next one slammed down onto her shoulder.

A merciful hoof plunged in through the back of her skull and she felt nothing more.

The cattle had swept through Horsehead, leaving broken porches, shattered plate glass windows, and a growing fire in their wake. Studying the carnage, Longarm was satisfied they wouldn't need to send the cattle back into the town. He and Ben dismounted, tethered their horses on fence posts, and walked further down the main street in the direction of the saloon. Beyond it, they could see the two blazing buildings—one of them the General Store. The flames were spreading rapidly to adjoining structures. In front of the livery the towheaded kid and his boss were hauling water from the trough and dousing the livery stable's wall.

Further down, gangs of men and even some women were forming bucket brigades to douse the sides of the buildings and prevent the fire from spreading. He could see men on the roofs hauling up buckets of water with which to dampen the rooftops, while overhead the sky was alive with flaring cinders. The smoke-filled air was becoming close, and it was getting more difficult to breathe with each passing moment. Longarm's eyes were stinging.

"Okay, Ben. We've seen enough," he said. "Let's get the hell out of here. Slattery must be on his way back by now. We don't want to miss him."

But as they started back to their horses, the sheriff, Dimmy and two other men appeared at the head of an alley and stepped out to block their progress. The four men had already drawn their weapons. Without pause they opened up on Longarm and Ben. Longarm flung himself into a doorway as Ben cut down an alley and disappeared.

The sheriff ducked back into the alley, but Dimmy was far more determined and led his two companions in a dash across the street. Keeping close to the buildings, they began to work their way up the street toward Longarm. The three men had Longarm outgunned. As they got closer their fire drove him back into a shop, and Longarm found himself in Jim Toohey's Tonsorial Parlor. Crouching behind one of the barber chairs, he held his fire and waited. The light from the flaming buildings gave the street a garish brightness, enabling Longarm to see anyone approaching the barber shop.

First one gunslick and then another stepped into view and peered into the darkened shop, unaware of how sharply outlined they were against the glow of the burning buildings. He waited until they stepped into the shop before cutting them down. Both men toppled to the floor. Longarm left the cover of the barber chair and began to unbuckle a gunbelt. He'd used up most of his cartridges firing over the backs of the stampeding cattle.

Dimmy stepped into the doorway. Longarm flung up his gun and pulled the trigger. The hammer came down on an empty chamber. Longarm flung the weapon at Dimmy, who ducked easily aside.

"You son of a bitch," Dimmy said. "I got you now."

"You think so, Dimwit?"

"That's the last time you're going to call me that."

Longarm threw himself to the ground and rolled over into a dark corner. Coming up with his derringer, he fired at Dimmy's darting shadow. His first round ricocheted off the arm of the barber chair. Dimmy flung a shot back at him, the bullet pounding into the floor behind him. Longarm fired back up at Dimmy and missed again.

Still behind the barber chair, Dimmy stood up and looked down at Longarm. In the dark barber shop, his yellow grin was barely visible.

"My, oh my," Dimmy said, chuckling. "That little ol' pea shooter's out of bullets, eh?"

Longarm didn't reply.

Dimmy stepped over the two bodies on the floor and walked around the barber chair until he was looking down at Longarm.

"Here it is, you bastard," he said, extending his six-gun. "Your comeuppance."

"Shut up, Dimwit and get to it."

Dimmy's grin got bigger. "Think maybe I'll start with your balls first."

Longarm was gathering himself to make one last, desperate rush at Dimmy when something black, tumbling end over end, crashed through the barber shop's plate glass window and sank deep into Dimmy's back. Dimmy turned slowly, astonished, and Longarm saw the curved lip of a crowbar protruding from his chest. Dimmy sank slowly, then dove forward to the floor, revealing half of Ben's crowbar protruding from his back.

Longarm got up off the floor just as Ben appeared in the shop's doorway. Ben looked down at Dimmy, a look of grim satisfaction on his face. Then he glanced over at Longarm.

"The sheriff's dead," he said, "so I thought I'd duck back here and see how you were doing."

"I'm glad you did," Longarm said as he bent over Dimmy's body and took the man's gunbelt. "Let's go. It's time we gathered up the men and rode back to meet Slattery."

Longarm ducked out of the shop, took one last look at the blazing buildings down the street, and hurried back to where they had left their mounts. Ben left the shop a moment after, his bloody crowbar thrust into his belt.

His few remaining riders strung out behind him, Slattery rode like a man possessed. Riding through that draw had almost wiped him out. The fire had come from all sides, peeling at least three more riders off their horses. One bullet had ricocheted off his saddle horn.

Well, this first round went to Long and the Lazy C, but as sure as bears shit in the woods, he would get even for this. Once he reached the safety of town, he would lick his wounds for maybe a week and let Emerald pamper him some. Then he would come back to the Lazy C, in broad daylight, no tricks; when he was done, every building would be in flames. He would have plenty of time later to build Em a new and bigger place.

It was close to dawn, but as Slattery rode he became confused. The light in the sky was coming from the wrong direction. Since when did the sun rise in the south? Looking closer, he saw how the light varied, brighter one moment, growing less intense the next.

Hell, that was no sunrise. That was a fire—a big one!

With an groan, Slattery realized what he was seeing. Horsehead was on fire! That son of a bitch Long had fired the town! But how could he have managed it? Slattery had left the sheriff and at least ten men behind.

Still riding hard, he saw with each passing second how widespread the glow was and how complete the devastation must be. Holy Christ! He had no place to go! The town could be wiped out!

The thought almost paralyzed him. For a moment he considered pulling his mount to a halt to get his bearings. Then he remembered that pack of Mexican riders still on his tail.

"Slattery! Look!" one of his men cried.

Glancing over his shoulder at the rider, he saw

him pointing off to his right. Looking in that direction, he saw a clot of riders topping a ridge. They were heading for Slattery and his men, fanning out as they galloped down the slope toward them. He was trapped. There were riders at his back and what looked like ten more coming at him head on.

"Keep going!" Slattery called to his men. "Blast your way through them!"

"Like hell!" a rider called, peeling off.

"Me, too," said another. "I've had enough!"

"Scatter!" cried another.

Looking back, Slattery saw his men sawing back on their reins so violently that the horses were rearing up, their legs pawing at the air. It was useless for him to argue with his men, he realized. As a fighting force they were finished, leaving Slattery naked. He yanked his horse to the left and spurred for the mountains.

Once he had slipped through the mouth of the pincers, he let up some as he climbed deep into the foothills. After a while, he looked back. For a moment he thought he was alone until he saw a single rider crossing a patch of moonlight. The shadow was visible for only a second, but Slattery knew who it was.

His nemesis. Custis Long.

Longarm came to a sluggish creek and forded it. Slattery's tracks were clearly visible in the soft sand bordering the creek. A few yards beyond the creek a swarm of deerflies attacked him with a virulent tenacity. He slapped furiously at them and continued into the foothills. Only when he had lifted high above the creek was he free of the persistent little bastards.

Slattery's trail led through a rocky patch of badlands. The grass was scarce, the mountain flanks sheer and tall, towering so high that in places they blocked out the morning sun. Slattery's tracks, meanwhile, remained clear, and Longarm was sure he was gaining on him. By midmorning he followed Slattery's spoor into a dungeonlike defile that turned and twisted like a snake, with overhanging walls so sheer and high that at times he could see no sky at all. The floor of the cleft was irregular, wet, sandy, and in places soupy from the streams of water that oozed through the multitude of cracks in the rock walls.

Meanwhile, Slattery's tracks remained as clear as newsprint.

At last the defile widened and he rode over a long section of caprock out of the defile and onto the floor of a narrow canyon. The stream that cut through it was only a thin, sluggish trickle.

And Buck Slattery's tracks had vanished.

Chapter 13

Longarm wheeled his horse and loped back toward the defile. A rifle shot rang out from the canyon rim, the bullet whining off a boulder. Once he had gained cover inside the defile, he dismounted and led his horse back over the caprock until he found an arroyo branching off it. It was filled with shale and great, broken slabs of rock that had peeled off the walls towering above it. Moving into it, he kept going until he came upon Slattery's horse tethered to a scrub pine. Beyond the animal was a steep game trail leading to the canyon's rim.

Longarm tethered his horse beside Slattery's, snaked his Winchester from its scabbard and levered a fresh cartridge into the firing chamber. Then he started up the trail, his feet constantly slipping out from under him as the loose shale and talus made a secure foothold difficult. The trail soon became so steep he was forced to pull himself up with infinite care. He felt like a fly on a barbershop wall and at any moment expected a blast from Slattery's rifle.

It was close to noon when, his knees and elbows raw, he pulled himself wearily up onto the canyon's rim.

As he moved off it toward a patch of rocks and brush, he caught the sudden gleam of sunlight on a gun barrel. He dropped to the ground as Slattery fired. The bullet whined past. Head down, he snaked closer to the rocks. Almost to them, he heard the scuff of boots on gravel as Slattery stirred behind a boulder to get himself more comfortable.

Longarm got to his feet and made a dash for a pile of rocks just above the boulder. Slattery heard his boots slamming the hard ground and stepped into view. He levered swiftly and sent a rapid fire at Longarm. As he ran, Longarm returned Slattery's fire. For a short while, the air was alive with hot lead. It stopped when Longarm reached the rocks and flung himself to the ground. Peering around a rock as soon as he caught his breath, he hoped for a clear shot at Slattery.

Slattery was not in sight.

Getting to his feet, Longarm descended cautiously to the boulder behind which Slattery had been crouching. Slattery's footprints were clear, as were the dark splotches of blood widening in the dirt.

He followed Slattery's tracks until he caught sight of him disappearing over the canyon's rim. When Longarm reached the spot he saw Slattery about thirty yards below him, moving swiftly down a steep game trail that clung precariously to the canyon wall. Slattery's entire right pants' leg was encased in a bloody sheath. Nevertheless, the wound hardly

156

seemed to hamper him as he clambered on down the trail.

Longarm left the rim and angled down the steep incline, tracked Slattery and fired, aiming at the rock face in front of him. It exploded in Slattery's face. The man cried out and flung an arm up to protect his eyes. Then he ducked behind a boulder. Longarm waited patiently and when Slattery stuck his head out from behind it, he fired again. Exploding shards of rock blasted Slattery's face.

Slattery ducked back and this time stayed out of sight.

"Bastard!" he cried. "You'll blind me!"

"Maybe you think that worries me."

"It's a stand-off. Let me go!"

"I didn't aim to kill you, just stop you. But it's no stand-off. You can't stay on that trail forever. So come up out of there with your hands up!"

"With my hands up? Hey, who the hell are you, anyway?"

"Deputy U.S. Marshal Custis Long."

"My God, you *are* a lawman! Emerald was right. Who the hell sent you?"

"Gus Coleman. Ever hear of him?"

"Sure. How is the old bastard?"

"Still thinking of you."

"He ought to have better things to do."

"He says your name's Jack Hawkins and you killed his wife and kid so you could get away clean from a Wells Fargo heist."

"That's right," Slattery admitted cheerfully. "And it worked, too."

"You admit it?"

"What choice did I have? That stupid bastard

Coleman came in when I was cleaning out the safe, him and his family. The stupid prick didn't have no sense."

"You mean it was his fault."

"I'm sayin' I didn't have no choice."

"You're telling me you *had* to shoot Coleman's wife and kid?"

"I knew he'd forget all about me when he saw them go down. Like I said, it worked. And hey, you didn't know that ball and chain he was married to. She had a tongue like a buzz saw, and the kid was a spoiled brat. I did that stupid son of a bitch a favor."

Longarm paused a moment. He felt as if he needed more air.

"Hey!" Slattery yelled after a moment, still keeping himself out of sight. "You still up there?"

"I'm here."

"Listen, if you're a lawman, you've got to come down here and help me back up. I'm wounded pretty bad."

"It didn't look that way a little while ago."

"There's a bullet in me, I'm tellin' you. I'll need a sawbones to dig it out."

"And I'm supposed to see to that, am I?"

"Hell, Long. I'm your prisoner now. You said it yourself. Come out with your hands up."

"We lost two federal marshals in the past two years, Slattery. They were sent up here after you. Know anything about them?"

"Should I?"

"Tell me what you know, or I'll leave you there."

"Hell, Long. No need to get your bowels in an uproar. There's really nothing to explain. We thought

158

the ranchers'd hired them to stop our rustling. We didn't know they was federal officers."

"So you killed them."

"Let's just say we left them for the buzzards. Them birds've got to eat too, you know. It wasn't nothing personal."

"You had the same plans for me."

"By all rights you should've gone under them hoofs like Pete Carson. You're a lucky man, Long."

"Are you coming up here with your hands up?"

"I told you. I'm a wounded man. I need some help."

"All right. Throw your rifle away and after it, your sidearm."

Slattery dutifully threw his rifle out from behind the boulder. It landed a few feet up the slope beyond it. Next came his sidearm.

"Hold on," Longarm said. "I'm on my way down."

He put his rifle on the ground and drawing his .44, picked his way down the steep incline to the boulder behind which Slattery was crouched. As Longarm stepped around the boulder and saw Slattery grinning as he shoved the muzzle of a Colt into Longarm's face.

Grinning, he cocked it.

"Just happened to have this spare," he told Longarm, shrugging. "Drop your gun, lawman."

Instead, Longarm bent and swept up a handful of dirt and gravel and flung it into Slattery's face. The man cried out as the sand dug into his eyes, ducked back and pulled the trigger. The shot went wild. His backward lunge had been so violent that he fell off the trail and landed on his back on a narrow rock ledge. Before he could grab anything, he began to slip down the ledge's steep, sloping surface. The gravel under his body went with him, carrying him relentlessly closer to the edge.

"Help me!" Slattery cried. "I'm going over! I can't stop!"

As he spoke, he flung his six-gun aside and started scrabbling frantically for something to hold onto. But there was nothing for him to grab. The rock was bare of all vegetation. As Longarm watched, Slattery slipped closer and closer to the edge.

"Get my rifle!" Slattery told Longarm. "I can grab it and you can pull me up. Hurry!"

Longarm retrieved Slattery's rifle from where the man had thrown it. Inching off the trail onto the sloping ledge, he held the barrel out to Slattery. Reaching out desperately, Slattery grabbed the barrel with both hands.

Longarm hauled Slattery up onto the ledge. Once the man was on his feet, he yanked the rifle out of Longarm's grasp and, grunting with the exertion, swung the stock against Longarm's shins with enough force to cut Longarm's legs out from under him. He crumpled to the ledge; his .44 vanished into the canyon below. Slattery steadied himself on the ledge and cranked a fresh round into the rifle's firing chamber.

Smiling, he aimed down at the sprawled Longarm.

"Why don't you try that trick with the sand again, Marshal?"

Longarm said nothing.

"See, Marshal, you don't have the stomach for your job."

"Don't I?"

"You could have shot me before when you caught me on the trail, but you didn't. You didn't aim to kill.

You just wanted to stop me so I'd come back up the slope with my hands in the air. Ain't that right?"

"I intend to take you in for rustling and attempted murder."

"Take me in, is it? And that's why you didn't let me fall just now. See what I'm sayin'? You're more interested in playin' by the rules. Hell, Marshal, you should've let me fall. What the hell am I to you? You just don't have no sense, mister."

Longarm did not reply.

"So now it'll be my turn. And mister, I ain't built like you. It won't bother me none to see you go over." He smiled, really pleased with himself. "And then Gus Coleman can spend another ten years huntin' me."

Longarm had fallen in such a way that his feet had crumpled under him. Reaching back to his right boot, he grimaced.

"I think you broke my leg," he told Slattery.

"Don't worry. You won't be usin' it much from now on."

Longarm squirmed as if he were in considerable pain, reaching into his right boot as he did so.

"Whatcha doin' there?" Slattery demanded.

But his question came too late as Longarm flung up his derringer and punched two holes in Slattery's gut. A look of pure astonishment crossed his face as he dropped the rifle and toppled backward off the trail. Longarm got to his feet. Slattery had rolled off the ledge and was hanging onto its edge, his eyes bugging out of his head in sheer terror.

"Hey!" he cried.

With a terrifying wail, he disappeared. A moment later his cry ended far below, its echo filling the

161

canyon for a long, eerie moment.

Longarm glanced skyward, searching its bright emptiness for buzzards. He saw one a great distance away, rocking like a cinder in the noon's hot updraft.

Satisfied, he climbed back to the canyon's rim, picked up his Winchester, and started back the way he had come.

Chapter 14

"Thanks, Rosita," Longarm said, mounting up. "But I've already spent more time here than I should have. Right now I've got to find a telegraph office or Billy Vail will think I've dropped off the end of the earth."

It was a bright morning and Longarm was leaving the Lazy C a more honest, but poorer spread. Not only had Rosita been generous in sharing her cattle with the Bar N and the Bench, but a few days before in Horsehead, with Longarm and Jack French at her side, she had sought out H. C. Billingsly and made it clear that the cattle dealer was not welcome and should not expect to purchase cattle in this valley again.

Jack French was at Rosita's side now. In fact, French was becoming a regular visitor to the Lazy C, and whenever Longarm came upon them discussing ranch business—or whatever it was they were talking about—Rosita had a tendency to blush and French to look uncomfortable.

"Well, I guess this is good-bye, Longarm," French said, reaching up to shake Longarm's hand. "The best of luck to you."

"Thanks, Jack."

Longarm touched his hat brim in salute to Eduardo, who was a step or two behind Jack French and Rosita. The old campaigner smiled, acknowledging Longarm's salute.

"Kiss me good-bye, Custis," Rosita said.

Longarm's saddle leather squeaked as he leaned down. French, somewhat embarrassed, stepped back. Moving up onto her tiptoes, Rosita kissed Longarm lightly on the cheek, then brushed his ear with her lips.

"Thanks, Custis," she whispered. "For *everything.*"

Longarm straightened up then and waved to Ben Smith and the wrangler, who were standing off to one side near the cookshack. In the bunkhouse that morning over many cups of coffee Longarm had already bid them good-bye and good luck.

He turned his mount, lifted it to a lope and headed out through the Lazy C gate. After one last wave, he headed southeast, eager to patronize once again the fleshpots and paneled watering holes of the mile-high city.

Gus Coleman's tired, squinty eyes regarded Longarm for a long moment without changing expression. It was as if Longarm's words had not reached into the man. The moment passed and Coleman slumped back in the booth's seat, his leathery face pale, colorless.

"Dead? Jack Hawkins is really dead?"

"I tried to bring him in legally," Longarm told him. "I could have hung a rustling indictment on him

164

without any trouble. Attempted murder as well."

"What happened?"

The two men had met in the lobby of the Windsor Hotel only a few minutes before. Vail had told Longarm where Coleman was staying, and Longarm had sent a messenger asking Coleman to meet him here.

Longarm shrugged. "What happened was that I deliberately gave Hawkins enough rope to hang himself."

"Why?"

"So I would have no choice but to kill him. I did fool, crazy things. Took chances. But it worked. At the end of it, I had no choice but to kill him."

"Then you had no intention of bringing him in to stand trial?

"I did at first."

"What changed your mind?"

"A remarkable conversation we had. He told me how proud he was of his crimes. He talked about your wife and child. I won't repeat what he said. It would be too painful. Then he admitted killing those two deputies. What he said was, he figured he had done the buzzards a favor."

"The bastard."

"As I listened to him, I realized he was a man without a shred of remorse for what he had done. There was a dark empty hole where his soul should have been."

"Yes. That would be Jack Hawkins, all right."

"Listening to him sickened me. But now I feel dirty as well. You can't be near such an animal and not be affected by the poison he generates. I've been trying to tell myself that I'm not as cold-blooded as

165

he was. But I made his death as terrible as I could make it."

"Jack Hawkins is dead," Coleman said. "That's the important thing. You have nothing to be ashamed of. Put that monster out of your thoughts. It's over."

"Is it for you?"

"Yes, I think so."

"Well, that's something."

Coleman took the hefty envelope file off the seat beside him and placed it on the table.

"Do you know what I'm going to do with this?" he asked, patting the bulging file.

"No."

"Burn it. With this file gone I will begin to live once more. Maybe it won't be as simple as that, but burning this file will be a start."

"Let's go out into the back alley."

"Why?"

"There's a trash barrel out there. I want to be there when you burn that file."

"Let's go, then."

The two men finished their drinks and walked through the lobby and out into the alley that ran behind the Windsor. They found the trash barrel and Longarm thumb-flicked a match to life. Carefully, they pulled out all the photographs, reports and indictments, every wanted poster, every scrap of paper that spoke of Jack Hawkins and his career and watched as each item flared up for a brief while, then curled into black nothingness.

When it was done, the two men shook hands and parted.

Later that night, as Longarm walked through the cool night on his way to a widow lady friend of his, he found himself whistling. He halted in his tracks to note the marvel, then started up again, feeling much better.

Like Gus Coleman, he was certain now that he would soon be cured of a malign spirit. Perhaps this night he would not come suddenly awake in a cold sweat, the scream of the man he had known as Buck Slattery echoing in his brain.

Watch for

LONGARM AND THE LADY SHERIFF

161st in the bold LONGARM series from Jove

Coming in May!

America's new star of the classic western

GILES TIPPETTE

author of *Hard Rock, Jailbreak* and *Crossfire*,
is back with his newest, most exciting novel yet

SIXKILLER

Springtime on the Half-Moon ranch has never been
so hard. On top of running the biggest spread in
Matagorda County, Justa Williams is about to become
a daddy. Which means he's got a lot more to fight for
when Sam Sixkiller comes to town. With his pack of
wild cutthroats slicing a swath of mayhem all the way
from Galveston, Sixkiller now has his ice-cold eyes
on Blessing—and word has it he intends to pick the
town clean.

Now, backed by men more skilled with branding irons
than rifles, the Williams clan must fight to defend
their dream—with their wits, their courage, and their
guns. . . .

Turn the page
for an exciting preview of
SIXKILLER
by Giles Tippette

Coming in May from
Jove Books

It was late afternoon when I got on my horse and rode the half mile from the house I'd built for Nora, my wife, up to the big ranch house my father and my two younger brothers still occupied. I had good news, the kind of news that does a body good, and I had taken the short run pretty fast. The two-year-old bay colt I'd been riding lately was kind of surprised when I hit him with the spurs, but he'd been lazing around the little horse trap behind my house and was grateful for the chance to stretch his legs and impress me with his speed. So we made it over the rolling plains of our ranch, the Half-Moon, in mighty good time.

I pulled up just at the front door of the big house, dropped the reins to the ground so that the colt would stand, and then made my way up on the big wooden porch, the rowels of my spurs making a *ching-ching* sound as I walked. I opened the big front door and let myself into the hall that led back to the main parts of the house.

I was Justa Williams and I was boss of all thirty thousand deeded acres of the place. I had been so since it had come my duty on the weakening of our father, Howard, through two unfortunate incidents. The first had been the early demise of our mother, which had taken it out of Howard. That had been when he'd sort of started preparing me to take over the load. I'd been a hard sixteen or a soft seventeen at the time. The next level had jumped up when he'd got nicked in the lungs by a stray bullet. After that I'd had the job of boss. The place was run with my two younger brothers, Ben and Norris.

It had been a hard job but having Howard around had made the job easier. Now I had some good news for him and I meant him to take it so. So when I went clumping back toward his bedroom that was just off the office I went to yelling, "Howard! Howard!"

He'd been laying back on his daybed, and he got up at my approach and come out leaning on his cane. He said, "What the thunder!"

I said, "Old man, sit down."

I went over and poured us out a good three fingers of whiskey. I didn't even bother to water his as I was supposed to do because my news was so big. He looked on with a good deal of pleasure as I poured out the drink. He wasn't even supposed to drink whiskey, but he'd put up such a fuss that the doctor had finally given in and allowed him one well-watered whiskey a day. But Howard claimed he never could count very well and that sometimes he got mixed up and that one drink turned into four. But, hell, I couldn't blame him. Sitting around all day like he was forced to was enough to make anybody crave a drink even if it was just for something to do.

But now he seen he was going to get the straight stuff and he got a mighty big gleam in his eye. He took the glass when I handed it to him and said, "What's the occasion? Tryin' to kill me off?"

"Hell no," I said. "But a man can't make a proper toast with watered whiskey."

"That's a fact," he said. "Now what the thunder are we toasting?"

I clinked my glass with his. I said, "If all goes well you are going to be a grandfather."

"Lord A'mighty!" he said.

We said, "Luck" as was our custom and then knocked them back.

Then he set his glass down and said, "Well, I'll just be damned." He got a satisfied look on his face that I didn't reckon was all due to the whiskey. He said, "Been long enough in coming."

I said, "Hell, the way you keep me busy with this ranch's business I'm surprised I've had the time."

"Pshaw!" he said.

We stood there, kind of enjoying the moment, and then I nodded at the whiskey bottle and said, "You keep on sneaking drinks, you ain't likely to be around for the occasion."

He reared up and said, "Here now! When did I raise you to talk like that?"

I gave him a small smile and said, "Somewhere along the line." Then I set my glass down and said, "Howard, I've got to get to work. I just reckoned you'd want the news."

He said, "Guess it will be a boy?"

I give him a sarcastic look. I said, "Sure, Howard, and I've gone into the gypsy business."

Then I turned out of the house and went to looking for our foreman, Harley. It was early spring in the year of 1898 and we were coming into a swift calf crop after an unusually mild winter. We were about to have calves dropping all over the place, and with the quality of our crossbred beef, we couldn't afford to lose a one.

On the way across the ranch yard my youngest brother, Ben, came riding up. He was on a little prancing chestnut that wouldn't stay still while he was trying to talk to me. I knew he was schooling the little filly, but I said, a little impatiently, "Ben, either ride on off and talk to me later or make that damn horse stand. I can't catch but every other word."

Ben said, mildly, "Hell, don't get agitated. I just wanted to give you a piece of news you might be interested in."

I said, "All right, what is this piece of news?"

"One of the hands drifting the Shorthorn herd got sent back to the barn to pick up some stuff for Harley. He said he seen Lew Vara heading this way."

I was standing up near his horse. The animal had been worked pretty hard, and you could take the horse smell right up your nose off her. I said, "Well, okay. So the sheriff is coming. What you reckon we ought to do, get him a cake baked?"

He give me one of his sardonic looks. Ben and I were so much alike it was awful to contemplate. Only difference between us was that I was a good deal wiser and less hotheaded and he was an even size smaller than me. He said, "I reckon he'd rather have whiskey."

I said, "I got some news for you but I ain't going to tell you now."

"What is it?"

I wasn't about to tell him he might be an uncle under such circumstances. I gave his horse a whack on the rump and said, as he went off, "Tell you this evening after work. Now get, and tell Ray Hays I want to see him later on."

He rode off, and I walked back to the ranch house thinking about Lew Vara. Lew, outside of my family, was about the best friend I'd ever had. We'd started off, however, in a kind of peculiar way to make friends. Some eight or nine years past Lew and I had had about the worst fistfight I'd ever been in. It occurred at Crook's Saloon and Cafe in Blessing, the closest town to our ranch, about seven miles away, of which we owned a good part. The fight took nearly a half an hour, and we'd both did our dead level best to beat the other to death. I won the fight, but unfairly. Lew had had me down on the saloon floor and was in the process of finishing me off when my groping hand found a beer mug. I smashed him over the head with it in a last-ditch effort to keep my own head on my shoulders. It sent Lew to the infirmary for quite a long stay; I'd fractured his skull. When he was partially recovered Lew sent word to me that as soon as he was able, he was coming to kill me.

But it never happened. When he was free from medical care Lew took off for the Oklahoma Territory, and I didn't hear another word from him for four years. Next time I saw him he came into that very same saloon. I was sitting at a back table when I saw him come through the door. I eased my right leg

177

forward so as to clear my revolver for a quick draw from the holster. But Lew just came up, stuck out his hand in a friendly gesture, and said he wanted to let bygones be bygones. He offered to buy me a drink, but I had a bottle on the table so I just told him to get himself a glass and take advantage of my hospitality.

Which he did.

After that Lew became a friend of the family and was important in helping the Williams family in about three confrontations where his gun and his savvy did a good deal to turn the tide in our favor. After that we ran him against the incumbent sheriff who we'd come to dislike and no longer trust. Lew had been reluctant at first, but I'd told him that money couldn't buy poverty but it could damn well buy the sheriff's job in Matagorda County. As a result he got elected, and so far as I was concerned, he did an outstanding job of keeping the peace in his territory.

Which wasn't saying a great deal because most of the trouble he had to deal with, outside of helping us, was the occasional Saturday night drunk and the odd Main Street dogfight.

So I walked back to the main ranch house wondering what he wanted. But I also knew that if it was in my power to give, Lew could have it.

I was standing on the porch about five minutes later when he came riding up. I said, "You want to come inside or talk outside?"

He swung off his horse. He said, "Let's get inside."

"You want coffee?"

"I could stand it."

"This going to be serious?"

"Is to me."

"All right."

I led him through the house to the dining room, where we generally, as a family, sat around and talked things out. I said, looking at Lew, "Get started on it."

He wouldn't face me. "Wait until the coffee comes. We can talk then."

About then Buttercup came staggering in with a couple of cups of coffee. It didn't much make any difference about what time of day or night it was, Buttercup might or might not be staggering. He was an old hand of our father's who'd helped to develop the Half-Moon. In his day he'd been about the best horse breaker around, but time and tumbles had taken their toll. But Howard wasn't a man to forget past loyalties so he'd kept Buttercup on as a cook. His real name was Butterfield, but me and my brothers had called him Buttercup, a name he clearly despised, for as long as I could remember. He was easily the best shot with a long-range rifle I'd ever seen. He had an old .50-caliber Sharps buffalo rifle, and even with his old eyes and seemingly unsteady hands he was deadly anywhere up to five hundred yards. On more than one occasion I'd had the benefit of that seemingly ageless ability. Now he set the coffee down for us and gave all the indications of making himself at home. I said, "Buttercup, go on back out in the kitchen. This is a private conversation."

I sat. I picked up my coffee cup and blew on it and then took a sip. I said, "Let me have it, Lew."

He looked plain miserable. He said, "Justa, you and your family have done me a world of good. So has the town and the county. I used to be the trash of the alley and y'all helped bring me back from

179

nothing." He looked away. He said, "That's why this is so damn hard."

"What's so damned hard?"

But instead of answering straight out he said, "They is going to be people that don't understand. That's why I want you to have the straight of it."

I said, with a little heat, "Goddammit, Lew, if you don't tell me what's going on I'm going to stretch you out over that kitchen stove in yonder."

He'd been looking away, but now he brought his gaze back to me and said, "I've got to resign, Justa. As sheriff. And not only that, I got to quit this part of the country."

Thoughts of his past life in the Oklahoma Territory flashed through my mind, when he'd been thought an outlaw and later proved innocent. I thought maybe that old business had come up again and he was going to have to flee for his life and his freedom. I said as much.

He give me a look and then made a short bark that I reckoned he took for a laugh. He said, "Naw, you got it about as backwards as can be. It's got to do with my days in the Oklahoma Territory all right, but it ain't the law. Pretty much the opposite of it. It's the outlaw part that's coming to plague me."

It took some doing, but I finally got the whole story out of him. It seemed that the old gang he'd fallen in with in Oklahoma had got wind of his being the sheriff of Matagorda County. They thought that Lew was still the same young hellion and that they had them a bird nest on the ground, what with him being sheriff and all. They'd sent word that they'd be in town in a few days and they figured to "pick the place clean." And they expected Lew's help.

"How'd you get word?"

Lew said, "Right now they are raising hell in Galveston, but they sent the first robin of spring down to let me know to get the welcome mat rolled out. Some kid about eighteen or nineteen. Thinks he's tough."

"Where's he?"

Lew jerked his head in the general direction of Blessing. "I throwed him in jail."

I said, "You got me confused. How is you quitting going to help the situation? Looks like with no law it would be even worse."

He said, "If I ain't here maybe they won't come. I plan to send the robin back with the message I ain't the sheriff and ain't even in the country. Besides, there's plenty of good men in the county for the job that won't attract the riffraff I seem to have done." He looked down at his coffee as if he was ashamed.

I didn't know what to say for a minute. This didn't sound like the Lew Vara I knew. I understood he wasn't afraid and I understood he thought he was doing what he thought was the best for everyone concerned, but I didn't think he was thinking too straight. I said, "Lew, how many of them is there?"

He said, tiredly, "About eighteen all told. Counting the robin in the jail. But they be a bunch of rough hombres. This town ain't equipped to handle such. Not without a whole lot of folks gettin' hurt. And I won't have that. I figured on an argument from you, Justa, but I ain't going to make no battlefield out of this town. I know this bunch. Or kinds like them." Then he raised his head and give me a hard look. "So I don't want no argument out of you. I come out

181

to tell you what was what because I care about what you might think of me. Don't make me no mind about nobody else but I wanted you to know."

I got up. I said, "Finish your coffee. I got to ride over to my house. I'll be back inside of half an hour. Then we'll go into town and look into this matter."

He said, "Dammit, Justa, I done told you I—"

"Yeah, I know what you told me. I also know it ain't really what you want to do. Now we ain't going to argue and I ain't going to try to tell you what to do, but I am going to ask you to let us look into the situation a little before you light a shuck and go tearing out of here. Now will you wait until I ride over to the house and tell Nora I'm going into town?"

He looked uncomfortable, but, after a moment, he nodded. "All right," he said. "But it ain't going to change my mind none."

I said, "Just go in and visit with Howard until I get back. He don't get much company and even as sorry as you are you're better than nothing."

That at least did make him smile a bit. He sipped at his coffee, and I took out the back door to where my horse was waiting.

Nora met me at the front door when I came into the house. She said, "Well, how did the soon-to-be grandpa take it?"

I said, "Howard? Like to have knocked the heels off his boots. I give him a straight shot of whiskey in celebration. He's so damned tickled that I don't reckon he's settled down yet."

"What about the others?"

I said, kind of cautiously, "Well, wasn't nobody else around. Ben's out with the herd and Norris is in Blessing. Naturally Buttercup is drunk."

Meanwhile I was kind of edging my way back toward our bedroom. She followed me. I was at the point of strapping on my gunbelt when she came into the room. She said, "Why are you putting on that gun?"

It was my sidegun, a .42/40-caliber Colts revolver that I'd been carrying for several years. I had two of them, one that I wore and one that I carried in my saddlebags. The gun was a .40-caliber chambered weapon on a .42-caliber frame. The heavier frame gave it a nice feel in the hand with very little barrel deflection, and the .40-caliber slug was big enough to stop any thing you could hit solid. It had been good luck for me and the best proof of that was that I was alive.

I said, kind of looking away from her, "Well, I've got to go into town."

"Why do you need your gun to go into town?"

I said, "Hell, Nora, I never go into town without a gun. You know that."

"What are you going into town for?"

I said, "Norris has got some papers for me to sign."

"I thought Norris was already in town. What does he need you to sign anything for?"

I kind of blew up. I said, "Dammit, Nora, what is with all these questions? I've got business. Ain't that good enough for you?"

She give me a cool look. "Yes," she said. "I don't mess in your business. It's only when you try and lie to me. Justa, you are the worst liar in the world."

"All right," I said. "All right. Lew Vara has got some trouble. Nothing serious. I'm going to give him a hand. God knows he's helped us out enough." I could hear her maid, Juanita, banging around in the kitchen. I said, "Look, why don't you get Juanita to hitch up the buggy and you and her go up to the big house and fix us a supper. I'll be back before dark and we'll all eat together and celebrate. What about that?"

She looked at me for a long moment. I could see her thinking about all the possibilities. Finally she said, "Are you going to run a risk on the day I've told you you're going to be a father?"

"Hell no!" I said. "What do you think? I'm going in to use a little influence for Lew's sake. I ain't going to be running any risks."

She made a little motion with her hand. "Then why the gun?"

"Hell, Nora, I don't even ride out into the pasture without a gun. Will you quit plaguing me?"

It took a second, but then her smooth, young face calmed down. She said, "I'm sorry, honey. Go and help Lew if you can. Juanita and I will go up to the big house and I'll personally see to supper. You better be back."

I give her a good, loving kiss and then made my adieus, left the house, and mounted my horse and rode off.

But I rode off with a little guilt nagging at me. I swear, it is hell on a man to answer all the tugs he gets on his sleeve. He gets pulled first one way and then the other. A man damn near needs to be made out of India rubber to handle all of them. No, I wasn't riding into no danger that March day, but if we didn't do something about it, it wouldn't be long before I would be.

LONGARM

Explore the exciting Old West with one of the men who made it wild!